Lightkeep

Magnolia Robbins

magnoliarobbins.com

Thanks for being a fan!
Happy reading!
♡ Maggie

The Sandwich

FROM THE MOMENT MORGAN Wallace introduced herself to Ms. Penny's third-grade class, Lily Taylor knew they were destined to be best friends. She was tall and lanky for her age, with frizzy dark brown curly hair and the biggest green eyes Lily had ever seen. It felt as if they could stare straight through you if she looked at you long enough. She wore a pair of well-loved sneakers and a hand-me-down jacket that had been used by too many people.

All Lily saw was someone who loved the water as much as she did.

"M-my name is Morgan," she'd said, nudging her glasses up onto her nose. She had a little bit of a lisp and stuttered slightly when she talked. "I-I just moved here from Seattle with m-my parents. I like the ocean, and m-my grandpa owns a lighthouse on the beach. W-when I grow up, I want to live in a lighthouse like my grandpa."

After she'd finished, Morgan came to sit down next to Lily at the adjacent desk. When she did, Lily smiled at her brightly. Morgan looked down at her feet embarrassed. Later, when they were working on their assignments, and Morgan's pen quit working, Lily passed her an extra. Again, Morgan couldn't look at her but thanked her quietly.

When lunch rolled around, Lily sat at her usual table, with her usual friends, getting ready to eat her usual sandwich. Just when she was about to take her first bite, she noticed that Morgan was sitting alone at a table across the room. Not giving it a second thought, Lily jumped from her seat and made her way over, sitting beside her. She couldn't help but notice that Morgan's lunch was rather small and unappetizing, to say the least.

"Do you want half my sandwich?" Lily asked her, offering a smile.

Morgan, who looked somewhat startled, stared at her for a long moment before she nodded. Lily tore her peanut butter and jelly in two and handed her the larger half.

"Thanks," Morgan said quietly, taking a bite of it. Once she'd finished, they shared a glance at one another. "I'm Morgan," she introduced herself, pushing her glasses up onto her nose.

"I'm Lily," Lily replied. She wasted no time speaking what was on her mind. "So your grandpa owns a lighthouse?"

Morgan smiled at her, taking another bite of the sandwich. "A-a big one! Right on the water."

"I always wanted to see a lighthouse."

Chapter One
Morgan

THE WALLACE LIGHTHOUSE in Kennebunkport, Maine was a sight to be seen. Two hundred and seventy-five feet, freshly painted a cream white and navy blue. It sat on the edge of a rocky beach, overlooking the Atlantic and its beacon shined each night faithfully for the boats in the harbor. Patrick Wallace had owned and ran it for nearly all his eighty years of living. Then, he'd passed it on to his granddaughter Morgan, who'd dreamed of having it since she was a child.

Lily, on the other hand, did not fancy the lighthouse as much as she did.

The fight had been going on for at least an hour. The two had just finished dinner when it had started to escalate again. "I hate this lighthouse!" Lily shouted aggravated as the lights flickered on and off in the kitchen. It had been the third time that evening. "I wish you'd just sell it already."

Morgan could feel her heart beating furiously in her chest. It had been months of fights nearly every night about one thing or another. Most recently, it was the state of the depreciating lighthouse that had become more and more of a burden as the months went by. Morgan knew exactly what the fights were really about but even so, she wasn't about to give in to Lily's demands. "We can't sell it," Morgan said, her hands buried in a sea of dishes in the sink. She wiped her face with the side of her arm before she continued working.

"You aren't listening to me," Lily argued with her from across the room as she resumed cleaning off the kitchen table. "We don't have the money for all this upkeep, Morgan. This place keeps getting in worse shape. The museum just isn't making enough. I can't support us both and keep throwing money away into maintaining something that's going to continue to fall apart every day."

Morgan pondered on what Lily had said for a moment. She wasn't entirely inaccurate. The place was old, and they had spent a lot of money trying to take care of it. It didn't seem to be getting any better. She hated being a burden on Lily, but she didn't have the heart to give it away.

"This place has been in my family for generations," Morgan finally met her gaze. She didn't look angry, just concerned. Even so, the two of them weren't bound to agree on anything. "I want to keep it that way."

"Well, you know *that's* never going to happen," Lily said flatly before she realized what had come out of her mouth. Morgan knew exactly what she meant when she said it. She could feel a small tinge of anger bubbling to the surface.

"I can't believe you're going to bring that up again," Morgan sighed, wiping her hands off on a tea towel by the sink. She put the back of her hand to her forehead.

"Well, you never want to talk about it," Lily noted as she finished cleaning the table top. After she did, she made her way over to stand beside Morgan and reached out to take her hand into her own. "I think we should at least talk about it."

Morgan pulled away from her, frustrated. "I told you, Lily," she said, "I just can't. Not right now. I wish you'd understand that." She could tell by the look in her eyes that she didn't understand and likely never would.

"Maybe if we could just get a real house, at least. Somewhere on the coast. Maybe you might change your mind."

Morgan sighed loudly, turning away from her to start putting the dishes away in the cabinet. She felt exhausted. "I'm not selling the lighthouse."

At that point, Lily seemed to break, throwing her hands in the air. She turned away, making her way into the living room and over to the coat rack. She pulled off her rain jacket and wrapped it around her.

"Where are you going?" Morgan watched her as she stuffed her boots on. When she turned towards the window over the sink, she took note of the sun sinking down into the horizon.

"To the boat," Lily replied curtly as she grabbed her keys by the door.

Morgan looked again to the skies, suddenly growing concerned. "Lily, I don't think that's the best idea. It's starting to get dark out."

"You don't think anything is a good idea," Lily snapped before she walked down the steps leading outside without another word. A few moments later, Morgan heard the door slam behind her.

There was a forbidding silence in the house for a while as she finished cleaning up the kitchen. The rest of the counters were wiped down, the floor was swept. As much as Morgan didn't mind a little bit of mess, she knew it made Lily anxious, so she did her best to keep things tidy.

Once she'd finished, she brewed a pot of coffee and sat down on the couch to read. Even with her busy mind, replaying the same arguments over and over in her head again, she managed to let herself fall into the book for a few hours. It was peaceful, and she found herself relaxing somewhat. That was until a loud crack of thunder rang through the entire house, shaking the walls in its wrath. The noise was so loud that it nearly made her fall off the couch. Concerned, Morgan made her way to look out the window. The sky had grown so dark she could hardly see outside. The rain pelting down made it all the worse.

Morgan waited for a few minutes to see if Lily would come back. When she didn't, she ran for her poncho and stuffed her feet into her rubber boots. The torrential downpour made her mood even worse. Why Lily had been silly enough to go outside in the dark and now in this terrible weather was beyond her. The rain made it nearly impossible to see. She made her way carefully down the path leading to the docks, expecting to find Lily's boat tied up. Instead, she became increasingly worried when it was nowhere to be seen.

The wind picked up, whipping at her from behind as she scattered onto the wooden slats of the docks. She studied up and down either side of the rocky coastline in search of the white vessel. Unable to see anything clearly, she grew quickly frustrated and made her way up along the edges of the rocks to get a better view.

"Lilly!" Morgan yelled loudly, though it would be nearly impossible for anyone to hear her over the rain and booming thunder. Her heart was racing so fast in her chest she thought she might pass out from the anxiety. Morgan walked down the very edge of the rocky shoreline where it was smoother. She tried her best to remain calm, though that was becoming increasingly difficult with each passing minute.

Just as she was about to turn and head back in the other direction, she spotted the boat. The front of it was nearly in shreds, caught up in the rocks along the shore. There was no sign of Lily. Morgan panicked, screaming into the night for her. She made her way carefully along the shoreline. As she neared the boat, she climbed up higher to get a better view. Her palm sliced into the jagged edge of a rock and she found herself bleeding. She ignored it, climbing until she reached the highest point above the boat.

As soon as she'd made it to the top, she saw Lily on the far side. Her body motionless, half in the water, half lying across the rocky shoreline. There was blood pooled around her and Morgan nearly lost her footing she grew so panicked. She cried out loudly as she moved down the rocks to get to her.

Morgan had never felt more terrified in her life than when she'd rode in the ambulance. She'd kept her hand wrapped tightly around Lily's the entire drive. Not once did she stir, her breath shallow and barely noticeable. As soon as they'd made it to the hospital, Morgan fled from the ambulance, racing alongside the gurney as they rushed her inside.

"She needs surgery," the doctor had told her as they wheeled her down the hallway. Morgan stumbled after her, only to be held back by a nurse who gently pulled her into a hug. She cried harder than she'd ever had into the arms of the stranger until she felt exhausted. The nurse sat with her until she felt the comforting embrace of a familiar friend.

"Oh sweetheart," Abigail said, letting Morgan's head fall into her shoulder. Even in her panic, hearing Abigail's sweet, tender voice could make anyone feel calmer. While Abigail held her, her husband Richard rubbed her back softly. Morgan sobbed for a very long time, unsure of what to do or think. Finally, when she'd managed to calm down, she lifted her head, turning to look at them.

"The lighthouse?" She managed to speak.

"We made sure everything was locked up for you before we left," Richard said, noting Morgan's slight panic. The minute they'd gotten into the ambulance, Morgan had called her neighbors, who, in her year of knowing them, had always been there when she needed them. "We'll stay as long as you need us to."

Morgan didn't believe she could last a minute on her own with the way things were going, but she nodded graciously anyway. Richard went to fetch her some coffee while Abigail stayed by her side. All the while, Morgan reiterated the events of the evening, crying in between bits of explanation. "It was such a stupid fight," she admitted when she finished, wiping her eyes with the back of her hand.

"Sweetheart, she's going to be alright," Abigail said as Richard brought her the drink. Morgan thanked him and sipped at it cautiously, feeling it warm her cold and damp body. As much as she wanted to believe those words, as convincing as Abigail was, she still found it hard to.

As promised, neither of them left Morgan's side. Mostly she paced the floor, unable to calm her anxiety-ridden body. When she finally was able to look at a clock, barely an hour had passed even though it had felt like ages.

Morgan jumped when she saw the sliding glass doors of the emergency room open. When he walked in, she met his glance. It had been a while since John had seen her last. He'd let his dark brown hair grow in a little bit thicker and sported a small amount of facial hair. Those intense gray eyes he shared with his sister hadn't changed a bit. He rushed to Morgan, and she hugged him tightly.

"She's in surgery." She was hardly able to speak. John nodded to Richard and Abigail before he sat back in a chair across from her.

"What happened?" The weather had obviously not let up by his frazzled state. Morgan reiterated the series of events that had led up to the accident, this time managing to get through it without erupting into tears. John sat silently for a while, trying to take in all the information.

"She's going to be okay," Abigail said again, reassuring them both.

The hours passed so slowly that Morgan thought she might lose her mind. Even amidst her worry, the three of them proved to be great distractions. Richard and Abigail talked about their bakery. John about his work at the bookstore he owned. Finally, Morgan spotted the doctor that had taken Lily back to surgery. Her hands braced against the chair. When he neared, John got up to greet him, shaking his hand.

The doctor met eyes with Morgan and sat down across from her next to John. "I'm assuming you must be Lily's family."

"I'm her partner," Morgan said weakly. "Is she okay?"

"Well, she made it out of surgery," he said, offering her a small smile. Relief flooded through her, at least temporarily. Until what followed next.

"However, I have to tell you, she's got a lot of recovery time ahead of her," he continued. Morgan felt herself sinking down into her chair. "She suffered an injury to her spine, and her head went through a pretty substantial blow in her fall. We won't be able to assess the full extent of the damage until she wakes. There were some other injuries as well, a sprained wrist, some lacerations, but comparatively, those are minor." Morgan did her best to nod. "All we can do is wait and see at this point."

John cleared his throat. "Can we see her?"

"Only immediate family, but yes. I can take you back to her if you'd like."

Morgan and John exchanged hugs with Abigail and Richard before they took their leave. "You call me if you need anything, alright?" Abigail said to her, kissing her on the cheek. "I mean it. I don't care what time it is, I'll be here in a heartbeat." Morgan smiled and hugged her once more before they parted.

The walk from the emergency room to the intensive care unit was the longest walk Morgan could recollect in recent memory. When they reached her bedside, she let out a soft cry and John wrapped his arm around her shoulders. She could feel him shaking when he held her.

Lily was attached to so many pieces of equipment, Morgan didn't know where one ended, and another began.

"I know it's a little shocking to see her like this," she could hear the doctor on the far side of the room. "Just know, all of this is keeping her stable. Now we have to wait and see."

Morgan sat in the chair closest to Lily, dragging it, so it was next to her bed. She wrapped her hand around hers, being careful not to tangle it in her IV. John came to sit beside her, and she could hear him taking deep, shaky breaths.

"She's going to be okay," he said, and it seemed as if he was reassuring himself as much as he was her.

The sounds of dozens of pieces of electronic equipment filled the night air with beeps and buzzes and chirps. Every tone made Morgan jump when she heard it. Her eyes barely left Lily's bed, watching her every breath. Tracking the heart monitor as the lines moved across the screen. Listening to the drip of her IV as it administered her fluids and medication.

Morgan and John stayed up for as long as they could. It was easy at first, with all the adrenaline coursing through them. Occasionally they'd take turns stretching their legs, but they were never gone long. Morgan eventually began fighting sleep. Finally, she laid her head down on the side of Lily's bed and found herself dozing off.

The next thing that Morgan recalled was being shaken awake gently by John. When she raised her head, she saw Lily, stirring. Morgan looked at the clock and realized a few hours had passed since she'd closed her eyes. She and John waited patiently until finally Lily opened her eyes and looked towards them. She let out a soft painful moan.

"Lily," John said softly, wrapping his hand around her ankle beneath the blankets. "You were in an accident. You're in the hospital. Everything is going to be okay."

Morgan wrapped her hand around Lily's and squeezed it in her own. For a while, Lily said nothing and just laid staring up at the ceiling. When she looked back down, her eyes were immediately on her brother.

"John?" Lily croaked. John nodded, while Morgan let her thumb stroke the side of Lily's hand. "What-what are you doing here?"

"I'm here for you," John said, doing his best to smile. "I came as soon as I heard."

"You're in the hospital," Morgan repeated John. "You had an accident, and you had to have surgery."

"It's going to be okay, Lil," John added.

"I-," Lily struggled to formulate what she wanted to say.

Morgan reached up to gently stroke the top of her head, being careful to dodge wires that were in the way. "Just relax."

Lily faded in and out of consciousness for the next hour. Every time she woke she was frightened, barely able to speak. Morgan and John took turns reminding her where she was and that everything was okay. When Lily finally managed to keep her eyes open, the doctor came in. He was an older man with salt-and-pepper hair and a greying beard. He had a kind smile and immediately went to Lily's side when he saw she was awake.

"Good morning, I'm Dr. Matthews," he said. "I see someone has woken up."

"W-where am I?" Lily asked again, dazed.

"You're at Southern Maine," he said before he turned on his light pen. "Do you know what day it is?" Morgan watched her as she pondered for a moment. Finally Lily shook her head. The doctor shined the light briefly into her eyes.

"Her pupils are responsive," Dr. Matthews noted. "Can you squeeze my fingers? As hard as you can." He held them out to her, and she did her best to wrap her hand around them. Morgan's worries grew worse when she was hardly able to. As soon as she'd laid down her hand, the doctor poked at the bottom of her feet with his pen. "How about this? Can you feel it?"

When Lily shook her head, Morgan watched her face grow panicked, and tears start to well up in her eyes. "I can't-I can't-." She was barely able to gasp for air.

"Lily, I need you to take a deep breath for me, sweetheart," Dr. Matthews said as he walked up beside her. Morgan reached out and took her hand, and John rested his back on her leg.

"Did-did you say I was at Southern Maine?" Lily asked when she managed to calm herself down. "What am I doing at Southern Maine?"

"You had an accident," Morgan told her yet again. "We had to take you to the hospital."

"Why did you take me all the way to Maine?" Lily asked, her voice panicked and confused. "I'm supposed to be in Seattle."

Morgan looked up at Dr. Matthews, gravely concerned. The two met glances for a moment before she finally got up the nerve to ask what she really didn't want to know. "Why are you supposed to be in Seattle?"

"The same reason you're supposed to be in Seattle," Lily replies, dumbfounded. "For school."

Morgan felt her body slip from the side of the bed as her hand released from Lily's. John managed to catch her before she tumbled to the ground. When she pulled herself together, she spoke again. "Lily, you've been living in Maine for a year now. We moved here after college. Remember?"

"What?" Lily stared at her, her face blank as it could be.

"Can I talk to you outside for a moment?" Dr. Matthews said, turning to look at the two of them. "We'll be right back." He gave Lily a smile and ushered John and Morgan out into the hallway.

"What's wrong with her?" John asked immediately after the door had been shut. The doctor took a deep breath and looked at them.

"We see this in some patients with traumatic brain injuries like Lily suffered. It's called retrograde amnesia. Where previous memories can become lost."

"She lost her memories?" John repeated him. Meanwhile, Morgan steadied herself on his shoulder, doing her best not to panic.

"Often they come back given enough time. We'll just have to wait and see. For now, you need to be patient with her. Try not to overwhelm her."

"What about her feeling in her legs and hands?" Morgan managed to ask.

"We'll have to take it one day at a time," Dr. Matthews said firmly to her.

John nodded, and Morgan did her best to follow suit. The doctor gave them a small smile. "I'll be back in a little while to check in on her. Let me know if you need anything." After he left, the two of them stood in the hallway, both trying to process everything that had happened. John scratched at his beard for a moment before he looked to Morgan. She nodded, and the two of them made their way back inside the room.

Lily was in hysterics when they entered. "I can't move my legs!" She sobbed, and Morgan rushed to her, wrapping her arms around her. John came to her other side, and the two of them sat on the bed.

"Deep breaths," Morgan said, running her hand over her head. "Deep breaths." After a moment her sobs turned into long rolls of air moving in and out of her body slowly. "The doctor said it might take a little while and we just have to be patient."

"What happened to me?" Lily asked them when Morgan broke away from her. John and Morgan shared a long glance at one another before Morgan proceeded to explain to her part of the events that had taken place the previous night, leaving out the details of their fight.

"So, I live with you? In Maine?"

Morgan nodded and looked at John.

"Oh God," Lily said, putting the back of her hand to her forehead. "I feel like I'm going to pass out."

"It's okay, Lil," John said, squeezing her shoulder.

"What's the last thing you remember?" Morgan asked her abruptly.

"I don't think that's the best idea-" John tried to interrupt her, but Lily pondered anyway. It looked as if she was struggling intensely to recall anything.

"Just being in school," she says, frustrated. "Dr. Connor's class?"

Morgan realized she was talking about their junior year of school. All the sudden she was filled with another wave of anxiety. "You don't remember anything after that?"

"Morgan, you're scaring me," Lily said, her breath starting to race again. "Oh God, I'm losing my mind." Morgan pulled her close and hugged her while John rested his hand on her back. The two of them sat with her, letting her cry softly. Eventually, Morgan felt her relax and realized she'd fallen back asleep.

"Who is Dr. Connor's?" John asked finally when they'd both realized she was out.

"A professor from our junior year of college," Morgan replied, their eyes meeting. "He taught a marine biology class."

"Morgan, that was over three years ago," John shook his head, unable to believe it. "Are you telling me she's forgotten three years of her life?"

"I don't know," Morgan stared at him. She certainly hoped not.

The Dance

FROM THE MOMENT LILY Taylor introduced herself to Morgan Wallace that day in the lunchroom, she knew that she loved her. It wasn't until their sophomore year of high school that she realized what that really meant.

Lily had begged for months for the two of them to go to homecoming dance together. "It'll be fun," she'd insisted. "I don't dance," Morgan had argued. The two had gone back and forth about it until finally, Morgan conceded. They'd picked out their dresses together and much to Morgan's displeasure, Lily had gotten them both dates.

The night of the dance the two agreed to arrive early to get ready together. John answered the door and directed her up the stairs to Lily's room. When she'd knocked, Lily answered, and she'd lost her balance when she caught sight of her. She was the most beautiful thing that Morgan had ever seen. She'd pulled her auburn hair up around her face, letting little pieces fall here and there. The makeup she wore was subtle. But the dress. Neither of them were the types to wear glamorous looking outfits, but that was the only word that even remotely described her.

"Wow," Morgan said, very aware of her disheveled state. "You look amazing." Lily gave her that killer smile of hers and drug her into her room. By the end of it, she had Morgan looking the nicest she'd ever felt in her life. Everything seemed to be going well. That was until their dates never showed.

They'd waited for nearly an hour. Finally Lily tried to call them, to no avail. John had offered to go over to give them "a stern talking to," but Lily talked him out of it.

"Let's just go to the dance without them," Morgan had suggested after Lily had a good cry about the situation.

"What?" Lily had replied, wiping tears from her eyes.

"I'll be your date," Morgan offered, holding her hand out to help her stand. The look on Lily's face was priceless. "Come on, it will be fun."

"But you hate dances," Lily argued as she stood up beside her.

"I like you," Morgan gave her a smile. "Now let's go before we miss it all."

John drove to the high school. "Don't keep her too late," he'd joked as they exited the car.

The two made their way into the crowded gymnasium, all the while Lily holding Morgan's hand tightly in her own. It sent feelings through Morgan that she still didn't quite understand but she knew without a shadow of a doubt that she didn't want her to let go.

They spent the entire evening together, dancing and drinking punch. Morgan let Lily gossip about the latest happenings on the dance team while Morgan told her all about debate practice. Even though they knew each other like the backs of their own hands, it was nice to talk, regardless.

Finally, as the evening drew to a close, a soft mellow song filled the room. Morgan felt Lily's hand slip back into her own and pull her out onto the dance floor.

"What are you doing?" Morgan asked, feeling very uncomfortable.

"Dance with me," she'd replied, wrapping her arms around Morgan's neck. The anxiety that had plagued Morgan her entire life boiled up inside of her. "People are watching," she'd wanted to say. Instead, she carefully placed her hands on Lily's hips, and the two of them began to sway to the music.

Morgan watched the others around them for a while, realizing quickly that no one really noticed or cared that they were dancing together. The thought made her feel instantly calmer. That was until she felt Lily's head lean down to rest on her shoulder. Morgan felt her body tense, but she did her best to keep breathing. She could smell the light perfume on Lily's hair and felt her breaths roll in and out of her softly. Morgan's heart beat so hard in her chest, she thought she might pass out.

At that moment, Morgan realized something that terrified her. Even amidst her fears and anxieties, she liked this feeling. Feeling her close. She liked it a lot. And it was at that moment that Morgan Wallace finally realized, she was, without a shadow of a doubt, in love with Lily Taylor.

Chapter Two
Lily

———

IT HAD BEEN A BEAUTIFUL Friday evening, on the cusp of summer. The sun was just starting to set, casting pink and purple streaks across the horizon. Lily and Morgan had brought the boat out into the ocean, having decided on taking a long weekend together. It had been Lily's idea. She'd planned it for a whole month.

The two set out off the coast a ways. They ate a picnic dinner together on the deck and downed a bottle of champagne. By the time they'd finished, the stars had begun to fill the night sky, stretching in every direction, like a beautiful glittering canvas. They were far enough off the coast that the lights didn't interfere much.

While the boat rocked gently in the calm waters, Lily's voice cried into the night as Morgan pleasured her. And after Lily had reciprocated, the two lay tangled together on the deck. They enjoyed the quiet for a while, holding one another until Lily looked into Morgan's eyes and remembered what she had intended to do.

As they sat up and Morgan pulled her close, Lily wrapped their hands together and smiled at her. "I've wanted to tell you something for a while," she said, and Morgan's big green eyes stared curiously at her. "Something I should have realized a long time ago, but I didn't."

"You're the greatest thing that has ever happened to me in my life," she continued, and she felt Morgan's hands squeeze hers. "I've never been happier than when I am with you. Morgan, I want to do everything with you. I want to grow old with you. I want to make a family with you."

She took a deep breath, steadying herself. "Morgan Wallace," she said, feeling her body quiver when she said it. Before she could finish, Morgan put a finger to her lips, and she felt the air slowly roll out through her nose.

"I can't," Morgan whispered back to her.

Every bit of oxygen escaped Lily. She could hardly breathe. "You can't?"

Lily knew the reason, without having to ask. A small part of her understood. The rational part that was buried deep underneath the completely devastated part that lie above it.

"We can make this work," Lily said, pleading with her. "Morgan, we can do this."

"Why can't we just be together? Why does it have to be marriage and kids and settling down?"

Lily choked down a small hurt cry. She pulled her hands away from Morgan, turning away from her.

"Lily, please don't be upset," Morgan said, placing a hand on her shoulder.

"We aren't your parents!" Lily pleaded with her, looking back into her eyes. "Can't you see that?"

Morgan stared at her for an awfully long time not speaking. She looked equally as frustrated as Lily felt about the situation. It was at that moment that Lily realized she was asking a lot more of Morgan than she was ready to give. That maybe all she needed was a bit more patience.

"I'm sorry," Lily finally broke the silence, offering her the best smile she could muster. "I understand why you can't. It's okay."

When the fight had happened that night two months later, it wasn't a big surprise. The real conflict between Lily and Morgan hadn't been the lighthouse. In fact, it hadn't been about any of the petty arguments they'd had as of late. Lily knew the reason they were barely holding it together. She knew the reason she woke up feeling angry so many mornings and sometimes found it hard to even look Morgan in the eyes was because of that night on the boat.

THE SUN WAS STARTING to set as Lily made her way down the path to the docks. She knew better than to go out alone when it was close to dark like this. Yet there was nothing that could tame the feelings that were burning through her insides. She knew the reason why Morgan didn't want to marry her or have children, but even so, she thought perhaps if she'd realized how much different her life could be with Lily, that maybe it would make a difference.

Lily untied the boat from the dock and then made her way on board. It took just a moment for her to start the engine and back it out. She'd decided to stay close to the shore. She'd take it around the coast once and then come back in. It wouldn't take longer than an hour or so.

Her thoughts wandered as the boat cut across the waters. She navigated almost mindlessly, having known it so well it was effortless. Before she knew it, there were storm clouds brewing. The air changed, and Lily began to grow a bit concerned. She turned the boat, heading back the other direction towards the docks. She'd gone further than she had meant to. By the time she'd gotten close, the rain had started to fall heavily, and thunder boomed through the night. It sent chills through her, and she pushed the vessel as hard as it would go back to the lighthouse.

The waves grew so choppy that the boat struggled to stay upright. Lily felt herself on more than one occasion fight to stand. The rain was falling so hard she'd lost sight of land. She pulled closer to the shore, quite sure she was nearly there.

Suddenly a wave crashed into the boat so hard that it sent her flying to the other side. She tried to catch herself but failed, and her head slammed into the metal railing. She felt herself roll onto the ground, stunned. When she managed to get to her feet, she felt a warm feeling trickling down her face. Her hand went up to touch it, and she noted that it was blood. Quickly she moved back to the helm, steering the boat as best she could. There was almost no way to see which direction it was headed.

By the time the rocks appeared it was too late. Another wave pelted the side of the boat, and she watched as it pushed at full speed towards the shoreline. Before she could brace herself, Lily flew through the air, slamming against the rocks and crumpling to the ground.

WHEN LILY AWOKE, SHE was lying against Morgan, wrapped in her arms. Pain shot through her entire body. Sounds echoed all around her. Her brother. Morgan. The beeps of machines. The world spun for a moment as she tried to get her bearings. Lily grew quickly confused, feeling her heart start to race and her breath quicken.

"Where am I?" She asked while Morgan sat up on the bed and moved to face her.

"You're at Southern Maine. You were in a boating accident. You're going to be okay."

Suddenly it came back to her. She'd just fallen asleep. A long breath of air rolled out from her, and she sat back on the bed. John's hand swept through her hair.

"How are you feeling?" She heard him ask beside her.

"Terrible," Lily admitted, trying to situate herself. The feeling in her hands had mostly returned, and she managed to squeeze them open and closed all the way. When she looked up at her brother, relief spread across her face, and he smiled. It still hurt to move them, but at least it was something. When she tried to rotate her right wrist, she winced.

"You sprained that wrist," Morgan explained, as Lily looked down at it. "They said it wasn't too bad."

Lily almost laughed at the comment. Everything felt bad.

As she attempted to move her feet again, the door opened, and Dr. Matthews stuck his head in. She felt her toes move ever-so-slightly and when he noticed, he smiled.

"That's a good sign," he said as he came up to meet her.

Lily watched as Dr. Matthews began to look her over. As he brushed his hand over the side of her swollen cheek, Lily let out a sharp cry of pain. It made Morgan and her brother jump in surprise. He moved his hands down to inspect her stomach. It was covered in bandages. He lifted one to inspect the wounds underneath, and Lily felt her body go numb and had to look away.

After he'd finished, Dr. Matthews made a few notes in her chart and then bid them farewell. A few minutes later a nurse dropped in to administer her some more pain medication. Lily felt it when it hit her, like a brick wall that instantly soothed everything. It wasn't long before she started to lose track of the room. Everything became hazy, and she found herself dozing off again.

When Lily awoke, she could recollect having a nightmare, but she wasn't sure what it had been about. Her brother and Morgan were asleep in their chairs, and it looked as though it was late in the evening. She sat quietly, staring around the room, looking at all the equipment attached to her. Listening to all the foreign sounds. Every part of her begged for this all to be a dream that she would wake up from soon and return to her normal life. A life that was full of classes and tests and homework. A life that wasn't stuck in a hospital with her best friend and her brother, having lost years of her memory.

It had to be a mistake. It had to be a dream.

Morgan stirred and soon after the two of them met eyes. She wiped sleep away with her fingers before she sat up and moved over to the side of Lily's bed.

"How are you feeling?" She whispered, running a hand over Lily's head. It felt oddly comforting, yet the way she did it made Lily feel strange. So much so that she pulled away prematurely. She couldn't tell if Morgan had taken offense to it or not.

Lily shook her head. "I'm alright," she said, though she was downplaying it slightly. Every part of her body still hurt. She concentrated for a moment on her legs and realized she still couldn't feel them. Yet her toes still wiggled some when she looked down.

"You'll be able to move them soon enough," Morgan assured her, taking her hand. "Just be patient." The two sat in silence for a while as Lily stretched her hands and arms as best she could, and wiggled her toes until she grew sick of it. Finally, she looked back to Morgan.

"This has to be a dream," Lily said, almost pleadingly. "Finals are in a week, I think. We were leaving for Maine for Christmas the day after." She felt herself fade off, her heart starting to race in her chest.

"You made all A's," Morgan said. "Even in Dr. Conner's class."

"That's impossible-I'm pretty sure I was doing terrible with subtidal ecology," Lily argued.

"I think there was one question on that entire test that had to do with it," Morgan replied. "He mostly tested us on deep-sea biology and the second half of the semester."

"How do you know that?" Lily looked at her baffled. Morgan's face dropped, and it looked as if she was unsure of whether to respond.

"Because it already happened, Lily," Morgan took her hand in hers and squeezed it softly.

Lily felt herself getting angry. A kind of anger she didn't recognize. An irrational anger that she couldn't contain. When she looked back at Morgan, her hand ripped from hers, and she glared at her, her voice elevating.

"You're lying," she snapped. "You're all lying. This isn't real. It's a dream. It's just some stupid dream, and I'm going to wake up any minute."

"Lily," Morgan started, but Lily couldn't stop herself.

"Get out!" She found herself yelling. "Just leave me alone, Morgan! Both of you!" When she looked at her brother, he was staring at her half asleep. "Get out!" By the time she'd finished, her voice was so loud, she was sure it was carrying into the hallway. Morgan and John both got to their feet and swiftly left the room. When they had, Lily erupted into a fit of sobs. Her heart was beating so hard that if it went any faster, it might have ripped from her chest. She couldn't stop crying. The length of her body shook violently.

When she'd settled into mostly heaving sobs, a nurse came into the room. She was young and likely new. It didn't matter. Her comforting arms wrapped around Lily's shaking body and held her close. Lily cried until she felt empty and hoarse. The nurse didn't let her go the entire time, rocking her softly. Finally Lily managed to tell her that she was okay and the nurse released her. Shortly after there was a knock at the door and Morgan and John peeked their head inside.

The nurse motioned to them, while Lily lay with her body leaning against her, still quivering slightly when she breathed. The two of them sat back in their seats, keeping quiet. Finally, the nurse moved away from Lily and stood up from the bed. She checked Lily's IV and looked at her vitals before she smiled and left the three of them alone.

It took Lily a moment, but she finally managed to look at John and Morgan. "I'm sorry," she said hoarsely. Morgan took her hand into her own and John wrapped his around her ankle. "It's just a lot to take in."

"Don't even worry about it," Morgan gave her a soft smile, shaking her head.

LILY SPENT SEVERAL days in the ICU before she was moved to a regular room. There was always someone with her. Most of the time it was John or Morgan, but there were a few occasions when John's wife Elise had come. The first time she had visited, Lily could hardly believe it.

Elise looked beautiful, slightly older than Lily remembered, but the same otherwise. With the exception that she was extremely pregnant.

"Wow," Lily said after she'd leaned over to hug her. Even with the small movement, she winced slightly. "When are you due?"

Elise had shared a look with John when she'd asked, and Lily knew she was trying to process the idea of her not remembering this fact. "Next month." Lily wasn't quite sure when that was, but by the state of her, she figured it was sooner rather than later. "We're having twins." Elise smiled and reached out for Lily's hand. When she placed it on her stomach, Lily could feel the gentle kick from one of the babies.

Unlike the ICU, the visits from the doctors and nurses trickled down a great deal once she had her own room. The week passed painfully slow being trapped in bed. By its end, Lily had started to become so agitated that she was nearly unbearable. She snapped at everyone, unable to control her temper. Finally, Morgan managed to calm her down enough to offer a surprise one afternoon not long after she'd arrived and taken John's place.

A blonde headed nurse came to get her. Lily had been waking from a nap when she'd arrived, toting a wheelchair. Lily watched her curiously as she came to her bedside.

"Ms. Wallace tells me that she thinks you need a little break from this hospital room," the nurse said smiling. Lily looked at her and Morgan. "Are you feeling up for it?"

Lily didn't quite think she was feeling up for much of anything given her circumstances. She still couldn't feel much of her legs, and her memory had yet to return. However, the idea of escaping the room, even just temporarily, was too hard to pass up. Finally, she nodded, and the nurse helped her down into the wheelchair. Lily hissed as she moved, feeling the pain from her injuries radiate through her body.

Once she'd gotten situated, the nurse wrangled her IV cord and unplugged her from her heart monitor. Afterward, she let Morgan step in behind her and take hold of the wheelchair. "Not for too long," the nurse said to the two of them.

"Can you hold this while we walk?" Morgan asked, nudging the IV pole. Lily wrapped her aching hand around it while she began to roll towards the door.

As drab and boring as the hospital was, Lily couldn't help but feel relieved rolling down the hallways. Morgan turned and headed down a walkway to a set of double doors leading outside. There was a garden on a hospital roof, thick with a variety of trees and plants. It was a beautiful sunny day out, and when Morgan opened the door, she was greeted with perfect late summer air. Lily breathed it in, smelling all the greenery.

"I found this the other day," Morgan smiled down at Lily as she rolled her out onto the patio. She parked Lily beside her as she sat down on a bench, admiring the view. On one end of the building, you could look out and see the ocean and the rocky shoreline in the distance. Lily couldn't help but smile.

"Thanks," she said quietly, still taking in everything around her. They were close enough to the ocean that there was still a lingering of salt in the air when she breathed it in. It was the most refreshing feeling in the world.

There was silence for a long while before Lily spoke again. "I still can't believe we live here." She was still filled with such disbelief, though the idea of it was becoming more and more real with each passing day.

"Yeah, a little over a year now," Morgan replied, looking at her. They hadn't really talked much about it since the accident. In fact, Lily barely knew any of the stories behind how she'd arrived.

"And we stay in your grandpa's lighthouse?" Lily asked, and Morgan nodded.

"Grandpa died our senior year of college," Morgan said, still looking at her. "He left me the lighthouse. You were the one who told me we should come back to Maine. We'd thought I'd take care of it for a few years and then start a volunteer program to run it. Then I'd come to work with you in Portland." Lily pondered on the idea for a moment.

"What do I do?" She finally asked.

"You're a biologist at the research center," Morgan said as she fiddled with the handle of the wheelchair. "You've been working there since we moved."

"I always thought we were going to be marine biologists together and live in Hawaii," Lily laughed, rolling the IV pole back and forth for a moment. Morgan smiled. That had been a running joke since their freshman year.

"Well, *you* wanted to live in Hawaii," Morgan corrected her.

Lily looked at her again and studied her for a long moment before she spoke. She could feel the heat in her cheeks when she asked. "And we're together? You and me?"

"Since the end of junior year," Morgan gave her a soft smile. Lily sat quietly, trying to wrap her mind around the idea. It just wouldn't sit, no matter how hard she tried to convince herself. She turned and looked out towards the ocean, watching the wave's crash into the rocky shore and listening to the traffic noise below them.

Morgan cleared her throat after they'd sat there a while. "I should probably get you back inside." It made Lily's heart sink a little in her chest, but she nodded anyway. She soaked in the sunshine for a few brief moments until she was surrounded by white walls and florescent lights once more.

By the middle of the following week, Dr. Matthews thought that Lily was well enough to be discharged from the hospital. She'd continue with home care and physical therapy, but her stitches were healing up nicely, and many of her bruises were nearly gone. Lily had started to get more sensation in her legs. While she still couldn't move them on her own, she at least was able to feel them again. Dr. Matthews was convinced with enough physical therapy, she could possibly be back to normal.

When Morgan had asked about her memories, it had been a different story entirely. "We'll just have to wait and see," he'd said to her. Lily didn't like his answer much at all.

The day she was set to leave, John and Morgan broke into an argument. They were standing on either side of the bed, neither of them acknowledging Lily's existence between them. It had gotten so heated they both had started to raise their voices.

"Morgan," John said. "She needs to stay someplace comfortable. The lighthouse isn't the best place for her to be right now."

"She's been living there for a year! Dr. Matthews said she needs to keep her routine. Living with you is not keeping her routine." Morgan snapped at him.

"There's no way I'm letting her stay there," John said. "Not until she gets better physically."

Finally Lily couldn't take it any longer. "Doesn't anybody care what I think?"

The two of them looked down at her, both suddenly growing quiet. She exchanged looks with them one at a time before she took a deep breath. "I should stay with John for now," Lily finally spoke, and she watched Morgan's face drop. She looked as if she might say something for a moment but then decided not to.

That afternoon, after Lily was finally discharged, Morgan and John loaded her into the car. Morgan buckled her into her seat belt. Just as Morgan was about to lean in and kiss her goodbye, Lily turned away embarrassed.

"What are you doing?" Lily said, panicked.

Morgan looked shocked for a moment before she realized. "Oh, I'm sorry. Habit, I guess." She gave her an awkward smile before she stood outside the car. "I'll see you tomorrow for breakfast?"

Lily nodded, having recovered from the incident and Morgan shut the door behind her. She and John talked briefly before he came around to let himself inside.

"Do you still live in our old house?" Lily asked when he situated himself.

John nodded and smiled at her. "It should be just the way you remember it. Not a lot's changed."

Lily found herself lost in thought most of the drive home. It surprised her how familiar the streets were and how she remembered the drive almost perfectly, yet it had felt like such a long time since she'd visited last. When they'd finally turned on the tree-lined street that she'd grown up on, it took her breath away.

"Wow," Lily exclaimed. "That view never gets old." When she looked at her brother, he was smiling.

"You know, you say that every time." John laughed, and she found herself laughing softly with him.

Elise made her famous shepherd's pie for dinner, and as usual, it did not disappoint. Again, Lily wondered the last time she'd had it. To her, it had been like she'd tried it for the very first time. She'd ate herself silly and enjoyed their company for as long as she could. After a while, she felt the pain starting to settle in again. John helped wheel her into the guest room, while Elise prepared her bed for her. It took the two of them to get her situated, and by the end of it, Lily felt somewhat humiliated and frustrated.

John knew how to lighten the mood. "Gee wiz kid, way to be a dead weight." Lily rolled her eyes at him but found it difficult not to laugh. When she did, it hurt her insides a little.

"Alright, get some rest," John said, offering her a kiss on her forehead. Elise gave her a squeeze on the shoulder before she left the side of the bed. Lily bid them goodnight, and they left her in the quiet darkness.

Even though this had been her room growing up, it felt as foreign to her as if she'd been staying in a hotel. She rolled slightly to her left, situating herself in a position that didn't feel terribly uncomfortable. Her eyes stared out the large glass windows across the room, watching the maple tree in the front yard blow gently in the wind. She could hear it rattle the windows slightly each time it passed.

The entire night, Lily tossed and turned, hardly able to sleep. Her mind was racing with thoughts. Something felt terribly off, and she couldn't quite put the finger on it. Whether it had been the strange feeling she had in her brother's house, the discomfort from her injuries, she couldn't quite figure it out. It wasn't until the sun started peeking through the window that she finally realized.

If Morgan was right, if they'd been together like she'd said, then Lily hadn't slept alone in ages. She laughed at the idea when she first thought of it, but her amusement quickly faded.

At close to eight, she heard a short knock at the door. Elise stuck her head in, and Lily rolled over somewhat to give her a smile. "Oh good," she said. "You're awake. Morgan's here. We were going to have breakfast."

John came to get her to the wheelchair. Elise ran a comb through Lily's wavy locks, and then the three of them made their way into the kitchen. Morgan sat at the table sipping a cup of coffee. She looked more exhausted than Lily ever remembered seeing her, even through years of stressful college classes.

"Hi," Lily managed to give her a smile, and Morgan looked up to meet her gaze. They both stared at each other for a moment before Lily finally looked away. John rolled her up to the table and then joined Elise to finish preparing the food.

"You look like crap," John joked to Morgan who scoffed at him.

"You could run a comb through your hair every once in a while," Morgan replied. She wasn't entirely inaccurate. Her brother's hair was sticking up in all sorts of random directions. Lily let out a little laugh, which then caused her to grimace when the sharp pain ran through her insides.

The couple had made a delicious spread of eggs and bacon, with a side of toast. John drank his usual cup of tea and ate all of his toast first, sans the crust. Lily snatched it from him as soon as he'd finished.

"Thief," he muttered, and she laughed.

After breakfast was through, Morgan took Lily back into the living room while John and Elise cleaned up. They studied each other carefully for a moment before either of them spoke.

"You look tired," Lily noted, looking away from her for a moment. The longer she stared at her, the more awkward it felt.

"Couldn't sleep," Morgan admitted, and Lily nodded, understanding completely.

"I thought I could come see the lighthouse today?" Lily asked with a small smile. "It's been a while since I-" She paused for a moment, realizing what she was saying. "I mean, I'd like to see it, if that's okay." Morgan's face lit up when she said it, and Lily couldn't recollect ever seeing her so happy.

An hour later they'd arrived at the gravel road leading up to the Wallace Lighthouse. It had been years, in Lily's mind, since she'd last seen it and it was far more majestic than she'd remembered. It towered into the sky, sitting on a rocky cliff. A small house was attached to it, and bushes and flowers lined the walkways.

"You did all the yard work," Morgan noted as she parked the car. "If you recall, I don't have a green thumb." Lily laughed when she said this. John had given Morgan a ficus to take with her to college. Somehow she'd managed to kill it within a week.

Lily looked impressed. "Well, I'm pretty fantastic at it if I do say so myself." Morgan smiled and exited the car to retrieve her wheelchair.

They spent most of the afternoon letting Lily reacquaint herself with the house. It was small, but it had a charm to it and was modestly decorated throughout.

"I tried to pick up before I came over," Morgan said as she wheeled Lily over to the couch. "Do you want to sit?"

"Can you show me around some more?" Lily asked her, looking up to meet her glance. When she did, Morgan beamed down at her and nodded.

The two wandered around the house, Morgan pushing Lily's wheelchair while she took everything in. Her hands brushed along the furniture. Every once in a while she picked up a trinket off a table and studied it for a moment, wishing desperately for a memory to come.

"This is our-the bedroom," Morgan said, correcting herself. "You picked out the sleigh bed. In fact, mostly all of this is you. You have an eye for that kind of thing."

Lily noticed a pair of paintings hanging above the bed and studied them carefully. They were the same painting. A beach scene. Except both were splattered over with paint of various colors. Morgan must have noticed where Lily was looking because she let out a laugh. "There's a good story behind those," she admitted, and Lily looked up at her. "You painted the one on the right, and I did the one on the left."

"When did I start painting?" She asked, looking up at Morgan.

"The end of our junior year of college," she replies. "We went to one of those paint night things on our first date and you were hooked after that. Those were the paintings."

A date. With Morgan. Again the thought of it took her breath away. Morgan must have noticed her awkward stare and quickly changed the subject. "Do you want to see your studio?"

"I have a studio?" Lily asked curiously as Morgan backed her out of the room and into the hall.

"We had a spare room in the back," Morgan said. "I made it for you when we first moved in. It was a surprise. You painted murals all over the walls and everything." As they turned the corner into the room, Morgan gasped. It was beautiful. There were windows on three sides, letting the afternoon sun inside. Across the walls, there was a magnificent painting of the lighthouse on the rocks and boats in the harbor around it. Littered on the floor were various works of art. Some finished, some just started.

"I think this is the only room you didn't care was messy in the whole entire house," Morgan noted.

"I'm not that bad of a neat freak, am I?" Lily said baffled.

"Lily, you have always been a neat freak," Morgan said, laughing. "I'm sorry to break it to you." Lily rolled her eyes as they backed out of the room and into the hallway.

The two of them sat in the kitchen while Morgan made coffee and sandwiches for a late dinner. When she brought them over to Lily, she split the sandwich down the middle, jelly and peanut butter spilling onto the plate. Morgan handed half to her and smiled. Something about the way she looked at her made Lily shiver.

"You know, this was our first meal when we moved in," Morgan said finally, just as Lily had finished her sandwich. "We had sandwiches and coffee and then fell asleep on the living room floor."

Lily laughed. "That must have made for a terrible night's sleep."

"We had a good time," Morgan smiled, pondering on the memory.

They were quiet again for a while as Lily finished sipping her coffee. As they brought their dishes to the sink, Lily finally spoke again. "I want to stay the night here if that's okay," Lily said finally, meeting Morgan's glance. Even though she tried to hide it, Lily could tell the idea made her genuinely happy.

"Really?" Morgan asked.

Lilly nodded. "I don't think I like sleeping alone," she admitted

That evening, as Lily wound down and was growing tired, Morgan took her back to the bedroom. She rooted through the closet and found a blue University of Washington t-shirt from college. It looked old and worn, but Lily recognized it the minute she saw it. By now it was nearly six years old.

"I remember that shirt," Lily said, smiling.

Morgan looked pleased. "I thought you would." The two of them sat in silence for a moment before Lily began to feel really uncomfortable

"Can you help me?" She asked when Morgan handed her the t-shirt. Morgan only hesitated for a moment before she carefully helped Lily remove her shirt and exchange it for the new one. Her fingers were careful and meticulous, watching every set of stitches and leftover bruises on her body. She was light in her touches, barely grazing over her skin and she did her best to divert her eyes while she helped Lily slip into the new shirt.

Afterward, Morgan helped her into the bed, slipping off her pants into some unfamiliar sweats that were supposedly hers. The style seemed like something she'd likely pick out, but it felt foreign. Morgan did her best to not make a big deal about helping her. When she'd finished, she situated Lily under the covers. For a moment, she sat on the side of the bed, the two staring at one another. Morgan reached over and gently brushed the hair from the side of Lily's face. It was such a simple thing to do, and it made Lily's stomach do flips the way it had been so effortless.

"I'll be on the couch if you need me. Just call." Morgan stood up to leave, and Lily found herself reaching out to grasp her wrist.

"Will you stay?" she asked, looking up at her. "It's just... I think I'd sleep better if you were here."

Morgan broke into a faint smile and nodded. Lily turned away as she changed into pajamas and a few moments later she had slid into the bed beside her. Lily took a deep breath, feeling herself relax when she heard Morgan breathing softly.

"Goodnight, Morgan," Lily said into the room. She felt her roll over on her side.

"Goodnight, Lily," she replied. Lily sat in the quiet for a while, listening to Morgan's light breaths and taking in the calmness of the house. She could hear the waves against the rocks outside, and it was far more soothing than the rustle of the trees from the night before. Eventually, she felt herself starting to doze.

Just before she fell asleep, Lily rolled slightly onto her side and pressed her back into Morgan's. It was subtle, only enough that she could barely feel her. Knowing she was there beside her was a comfort she couldn't explain, and it only took moments before she was able to drift deep into sleep.

The Cherry Blossom Tree

THE FIRST TIME THAT Lily Taylor realized that Morgan Wallace was in love with her was underneath the shade of a cherry blossom tree. It had been a nice spring day. The sun was shining enough that you didn't get a chill from the wind, but it was still brisk enough to wear a light jacket. A perfectly pleasant Seattle day to be outside.

Every year since they'd moved for college, Morgan and Lily would go to the Cherry Blossom Festival downtown. This particular year, the crowds were thick. While Lily enjoyed being surrounded by people and the bustle of city life, it often times made Morgan nervous. So after a brief walk through the booths and happenings, Lily took her hand, and the two of them wandered away from the masses and into the park nearby.

As soon as they'd broken from the crowd, Lily could see Morgan's posture relax a bit, and the tense look on her face dissipate. It was as if she became an entirely different person. They met eyes and Morgan smiled at her. While they walked, their hands still clasped together in a friendly sort of way, Morgan swung their arms back and forth lightly.

"Are you going back home for spring break?" Morgan finally asked her after they'd traveled in silence for a while. She broke their hands apart then and the instant she had, she felt part of her regret it. There was something nice about it that she couldn't explain.

"I don't know," Lily admitted. It would be nice to see John but leaving for college had been the best thing she'd ever done since the accident. Hardly a day went by that she didn't think about it and it only was worse when she was at home. When she finally shook the thoughts from her head, she was about to ask Morgan the same question when she realized the answer would likely be the same.

"We should go on a trip together," Morgan thought aloud. "Somewhere on the coast. Maybe Portland? San Diego?"

"I've always wanted to go to San Diego," Lily said thoughtfully.

They'd reached the cherry blossoms. It was slightly windy, so their petals fell in small batches towards the ground. The two of them stood, overlooking the crowd below them. When Lily turned to look back at Morgan, she found her staring at her intensely.

"What?" Lily asked, finding it hard to keep her eyes on her. Every time Morgan looked at you like that, it felt as if she was staring right into your soul. Those big green eyes filled with such raw, unfiltered emotion.

Morgan reached out towards Lily's face then, plucking a petal from her hair and twirling it in her fingers.

"I love you," she said when they met eyes again. Lily felt something fill her to the brim. Something that made her heart race and her breath quicken. The way she looked at her... Lily hadn't ever seen her look that way before.

"I love you too," Lily replied, unsure of what to say other than that. It was the habitual kind of thing you would say in response. Not anything like the way Morgan had just spoken to her.

The two sat on the ground together, people watching in silence. All the while, Lily's mind raced, thinking about what Morgan had said. It hadn't been a simple reminder of their friendship. What she had said ran much deeper than that. Lily had suspected for a long time that there was something that she had been missing. She never knew what exactly it was. Not until that moment.

Chapter Three
Morgan

IT WAS EARLY. MORGAN had forgotten to set her alarm, but after a year, her body had grown accustomed to her routine. When she'd managed to open her eyes, she realized that Lily was curled up beside her, sleeping soundly, one of Morgan's arms resting on her side. Morgan laid there for a moment, enjoying the feeling of her closeness. She couldn't remember the last time that Lily had let her hold her while she slept. Months at least. Ever since the incident on the boat.

Morgan struggled for a long while to force herself out of bed. She carefully removed her arm from Lily, trying her best to not disturb her peaceful slumber. When she'd successfully pulled away, she made her way to the closet to change. Just as she finished, she heard the sheets rustle.

"What time is it?" Lily asked her in the darkness.

Morgan turned around to look at her in the faint moonlight shining through the window. "Early," she replied. "Go back to sleep."

"What are you doing up?" Lily inquired, rolling herself over slightly. Morgan heard her yelp in pain before she settled into the bed. She looked at the clock and yawned as she did. "It's six in the morning." The sun was just starting to peek over the horizon.

"I always get up this early," Morgan replied. "Lightkeeper duties." There was a long silence in the room while Lily pondered over what was said. Finally, Morgan realized that she likely didn't know what she meant. "Lighthouse chores," she corrected herself.

"Can I watch?" She asked, almost immediately. Morgan was taken aback by her enthusiasm. Lily hadn't wanted anything to do with the lighthouse in months, and even before their fight, Morgan usually got up on her own. "Please?"

Morgan, who was still trying to come to terms with the fact that this was an entirely different Lily than she'd known weeks prior, finally managed to nod. "Okay."

After carefully loading her into the wheelchair, Morgan pushed Lily out into the living room. They moved swiftly over to the doors that lead out onto the porch outside. When she opened them, the misty wind bit at her. Lily shivered, and Morgan went to fetch the throw off of the couch and wrapped it around her.

"Thanks," Lily smiled at her as she was wheeled out onto the deck.

"The first thing I do is raise the flag," Morgan said as she walked out onto the deck. She unraveled the cord and pulled until it reached the top. When she turned back to Lily, she was looking up at it curiously. "It's mostly just for tradition."

They went back into the house, and Morgan took her to the door leading up into the actual lighthouse. Before Lily could ask, Morgan reached down and scooped her out of the wheelchair after she'd opened the door. Lily wrapped her arms around her neck, and the two proceeded up the curving steps to the top.

"You smell," Lily noted and Morgan almost dropped her midway up the steps. She could feel her cheeks getting red. "I'm just kidding," Lily laughed. Morgan resumed walking, shaking her head. Lily definitely had the same sense of humor as her brother, that was for certain. By the time Morgan had reached the top, she was nearly out of breath.

Lily gasped softly as she looked around. "Wow," she said as Morgan made a loop around the perimeter, still holding on to her. The two admired the scenery for a moment. You could see the ocean and the rocky shoreline nearly all the way around the building. The early morning light was just starting to spread across the horizon. Finally, Morgan sat Lily down against the wide lip of the window. She pulled the cleaning supplies out of the cabinet by the steps and proceeded to wipe down the reflective panels in the center of the room. For a while, they were both quiet as she worked.

"Did the light bother you last night while you were sleeping?" Morgan asked as she finished up.

Lily shook her head. "I didn't even notice it," she admitted. Morgan found this funny since it had used to be one of the very long list of complaints she had about the lighthouse. "Do you do this every morning?" She asked. Morgan nodded. "You must really love this place."

Morgan couldn't help but smile when she said it.

"What?" Lily asked curiously at her as she put away the cleaning supplies.

Morgan hesitated for a moment, wondering if she should even bring it up. "I know you don't remember, but you hate this lighthouse." Lily's eyes grew wider, and she let out a little laugh.

"Why on Earth would I hate this lighthouse? It's amazing."

"It's falling apart," Morgan said as she went to pick her up again. Lily wrapped her arms around Morgan's neck, and she held onto her carefully. By the look on her face, she looked like she was in pain, but she didn't say anything about it.

"Then we should fix it," Lily argued. It took her a moment to realize what she had said, and Morgan watched her turn away, embarrassed. They didn't speak again until they'd reached the bottom of the staircase and Morgan had put her back in her wheelchair.

"What next?" Lily asked, looking up at her.

The two spent the early morning doing a variety of chores. Morgan showed her how to use the radio, and she talked to a few of owners of the boats out in the harbor. After breakfast, they made their way out to the museum building that was adjacent to the lighthouse.

"So you run the museum?" Lily asked her as she pushed the wheelchair along the concrete pathway.

"Since we got here last year," Morgan replied, pulling out the keys to unlock the door. For being such a small place, her grandfather had made a fine museum. In the center was a full-scale replica of the lighthouse, made by Patrick himself. His old rowboat beside it. There were cases of old mementos that had been washed up on the shores over the years.

Morgan led Lily around the room, letting her have a look at everything. She watched her closely as her hands ran over the replica and the boat. She studied the collections as if they were the most interesting things in the entire world. When they'd finished, Morgan brought her back up to the front and let her sit at the counter as she tidied up the place.

The rest of the morning Morgan toted Lily around while she finished her chores. Whenever there was something Lily was able to help with, she pitched in. By the early afternoon, Morgan could tell by the way she was acting that pain had set in. John showed up a little after lunch in preparation to take Lily to her first physical therapy appointment.

"I don't think she should be over-extending herself," he said to Morgan as the two of them watched her wash the dishes from lunch in the sink. There had been a debate about it beforehand, but she had insisted.

"She wanted to," Morgan replied as she and John met glances. After Lily finished cleaning off the dishes, she turned the wheelchair around to face them. Again, Morgan saw the tiredness in her eyes, but she didn't complain.

John and Morgan helped load Lily into his car, and the three of them set off to Portland for her appointment. Morgan kept an eye on her from the back as they drove. Lily's eyes were wistful as they watched out the window. Every month through their high school years, Lily, John, and Morgan would travel to Portland for the day to eat and play on the beaches. In the winter, they'd go to ice skate and drink hot chocolate. It had been a tradition. As they drove down the highway, Morgan couldn't help but reminisce about those times.

Portland, Maine was a beautiful coastal city north of Kennebunkport. It was older, with brick buildings and a harbor that was nearly always full of boats. The drive took them right along the edges of the rocky beaches. The three were quiet as they rode along, admiring the scenery.

As they situated Lily into her wheelchair, Morgan couldn't help but notice the prying eyes of strangers as they walked by. Lily looked oddly uncomfortable. John seemed to notice too and wasted no time lightening the mood.

"Hey Lil," he said, leaning down to whisper to her as they rolled her towards the building. "What do you call bees that produce milk?"

Lily looked up at him for a moment, not amused. He leaned down and whispered something in her ear and when he did her face erupted in a smile. She shoved him playfully and rolled her eyes.

"That was terrible," she laughed, and John looked pleased.

CARMELA DANG COULD have been deemed one of the nicest souls on the planet. She was a tiny petite physical therapist from Vietnam. Her husband Tom worked alongside her as an occupational therapist. Morgan couldn't think of any two people who seemed to love their jobs more than they did and they were bound and determined to help Lily in any way possible.

"Alright, Lily," Carmela clapped her hands together as the two of them met eyes. Tom had just finished helping her lie on a table. When he was through, Carmella moved up to gently hold on to one of her legs. "We're going to stretch you out a little bit first, okay?" Morgan watched as she moved her legs one at a time.

"Can you tell me if you feel anything?" Carmela asked her while she worked.

Lily shook her head, and Morgan could see the frustrated look in her eyes. "Just a little," she replied, grimacing slightly when her legs were moved a certain direction.

"Can you try to move your toes for me?" Carmela asked. Morgan watched Lily focus on her feet as hard as she could and managed to move them slightly. "Good!" Carmela beamed at her.

While Tom and Lily worked together on some mobility exercises, Carmela took Morgan and John outside of the room to talk.

"When is her next doctor's appointment?" Carmela asked them.

"Next week," Morgan said as John was reaching for his phone to check. "Tuesday. With Dr. Matthews."

"Has he talked to you about her leg function at all?" Carmela glanced at them. The way she asked the question gave Morgan a very bad feeling in the pit of her stomach. She shook her head, and Carmela continued. "Now, I'm not her doctor, so I don't have much say in the matter. But I just wanted to prepare you."

"Prepare us for what, exactly?" John asked, crossing his arms over his chest. Morgan leaned against the wall quietly, unsure if she wanted to hear the answer to that question.

"It's hard to tell with spinal cord injuries the extent of the damage and whether or not a person will regain full function again. It may take Lily months, if not years to gain mobility back. And she may never recover all of her leg function."

Even though Morgan knew this could be the case, it was still hard to hear it. By the look on John's face, he wasn't any more thrilled about the news. They both nodded, and Carmela smiled softly at them.

"The good news is, she has some function in her legs already. So we'll do the best we can. All you can do now is just keep encouraging her and stay positive."

After the therapy session, John treated Morgan and Lily to an early dinner at a seafood restaurant on the coast. In spite of the conversation he and Morgan had with Carmela, they both did their best to remain positive on their outing. The restaurant they'd used to go to many years ago had closed, so they'd picked a place down the street. The food was good, the ambiance better. John sipped on tea and shared his french fries with Lily, who insisted upon stealing one every few minutes.

On the drive home, Lily sat in the back next to Morgan. It had started to grow dark outside, and before she knew it, Morgan found Lily lying with her head on her shoulder, fast asleep. John looked in the rearview mirror at the two of them, and Morgan shrugged. Once again she found herself enjoying Lily's affection, even if it was purely platonic. She'd missed it. Craved it even.

"Do you think she'll remember anything?" Morgan finally asked John, quietly, as to not disturb Lily.

John took a long moment to respond. "I don't know."

"John, I don't know if she's ever going to feel the same way about me again if she doesn't. I mean, it was a wonder she did in the first place."

Again, John thought for a long while before he said anything. "You know, my dad always used to be a big believer in that 'everything happens for a reason' type of thing. I always thought he was crazy for thinking it. Especially after what happened to them, and now what happened to Lily." He paused for a moment, thinking again. "Sometimes I don't think he was wrong though. At least, I don't think he meant wrongly by it. I mean, life is filled with all of these possible reasons for everything. Why not choose to believe that there's a reason for why things happen?"

"So I'm just supposed to believe that Lily's accident was supposed to happen?"

"I'm saying," John says, glancing at her again. "That maybe you can find a way to be at peace with it, no matter the reason why it happened. Trust that things will work out the way that they need to work out."

Morgan didn't much like his answer, but she couldn't find anything to say in response. Instead, they rode in silence most of the rest of the way back.

As they turned onto the gravel driveway at the lighthouse, Lily was still fast asleep. John came to help carry her up the steps into the house. He laid her on the couch, kissing her softly on her forehead before he said his quiet goodbyes to Morgan.

While she rested, Morgan tidied the kitchen and went out to make sure things in the lighthouse were in order. As she walked back inside, she noticed Lily watching her.

"Go back to sleep," Morgan said quietly to her as she shut the door behind her.

Lily stifled a yawn. "I think I need a shower if that's okay."

Without a moment's hesitation, Morgan went to fetch her from the couch, carrying her down the hallway to the bathroom. She set her on the countertop, letting her back lay against the wall mirror. Lily watched her carefully as she set up the shower for her. There was a small stool the hospital had given them when they'd left for her to sit on. Morgan arranged the soaps in such a way that they were easily accessible and then turned back to face her.

The two made a silent agreement before Morgan went to help her undress. Her hands swept under Lily's shirt, letting it fall to the floor. Once it had, Morgan looked her over for a moment, checking her bruises and the places they had stitched along her abdomen. With careful fingers, Morgan traced along her wounds, careful not to press down too hard. Even her gentle touch made Lily wince slightly.

"Sorry," Morgan apologized, moving her hand away. "It looks like you're healing well." Lily nodded in agreement as Morgan began to undress her the rest of the way. Lily pushed with her arms to raise her lower body up as Morgan slid the bottom half of her clothing off in one fell swoop. When they met eyes, Morgan could tell Lily was holding back frustration.

"You just have to be patient," Morgan assured Lily as she scooped her up and carried her to the stool. Lily balanced herself against the side of the tile wall while Morgan started the water. Once it was warm enough, she slid her underneath the spray. She was too focused on making sure she was comfortable to mind her nakedness.

"Are you alright?" Morgan asked as she stepped back out of the shower. Lily nodded, quieter than she normally was. "I'll be right outside if you need me. Let me know when you're through." Lily nodded again, not speaking, and Morgan took that as her cue to leave.

Once she was outside, Morgan laid her body against the wall in the hallway and felt herself slowly slide down it to the floor. She rested her elbows on her knees and buried her face in her hands. So many emotions flooded through her at that moment, it made it hard for her to breathe. She thought about what John had said in the car. About accepting things that happen. It made her laugh out loud slightly. Morgan didn't think she could ever accept this situation.

As her thoughts began to wander off, Morgan heard a loud thud from the inside of the bathroom. It vibrated the floor. Shortly after, she could hear Lily sobbing. Morgan rushed to her feet faster than she ever had and quickly made her way back into the room. Lily laid sprawled out on the floor of the shower, having fallen off the stool. Just as Morgan entered she let out a frustrated cry and threw the bottle of shampoo at the wall.

Morgan didn't think. She moved quickly into the shower, falling behind Lily. The water pooled around her, soaking through her clothes and drenching her hair. Both of her arms wrapped around Lily tightly, pulling her close and holding her arms to her body. Morgan rested her chin on the top of Lily's head while she rocked her softly, shushing her.

"Everything's okay," Morgan whispered to her. Lily didn't argue, she only cried. After a while, she managed to catch her breath. When she did, Morgan turned her around so that the back of her head faced towards the water. The two sat, letting the stream fall down over them, while Morgan ran her fingers through Lily's hair, washing out the remnants of soap that lie there. She worked gently and calmly, watching as Lily's eyes closed and her body relaxed somewhat.

When she finished, Morgan sat her against the wall of the shower and reached under her chin to tilt her head up a little. When Lily finally looked at her, Morgan couldn't help but smile softly. Her eyes were red and puffy, and she looked as miserable as she could be, but it was the look of the Lily she'd loved all her life. Those beautiful soft grey eyes staring deeply at her.

"I'm never going to walk again," Lily let out a soft sob, and Morgan stroked her chin with her thumb before she leaned in and kissed her on the forehead.

"We'll figure it out," Morgan said, brushing her hand against her cheek. The water from the shower rolled down her face and onto her sopping wet clothes. They were quiet for a while, Lily sniffling and taking in deep breaths. When Lily and Morgan met eyes again, they stared at each other intensely.

Morgan reacted before she could stop herself. She moved in one fluid motion, pressing their lips tightly together. Morgan breathed her in as if it were the first time they'd ever kissed. Lily pushed back into her and Morgan felt as Lily weaved her fingers into her wet curls. Tasted the water that rolled between their lips when they'd part just for a moment. They stayed together for a long while, but it hardly felt like seconds to Morgan.

The two stared at each other awkwardly when they finally pulled away. Finally, Morgan helped her off the ground and sat her on the counter again. After Morgan changed into dry clothes, she fetched a towel and helped dry her off. Lily could barely look at her the entire time. After they'd managed to get her into a fresh set of clothes, Morgan decided to speak.

"Lily," she started, but it was quickly interrupted by the last thing on Earth that she had wanted to hear.

"I think I need to stay with John," Lily said, clearing her throat. "It would be better that way."

Morgan met eyes with her just for a moment before she looked away. "Is that really what you want? Wouldn't you rather stay here with me? This is your home." Morgan let her hand fall gently on Lily's shoulder.

"This isn't my home!" Lily snapped, pulling herself away. "I don't know what this is. I haven't been here since I was a child. All I know is that I'm supposed to be in Seattle right now. Not in Maine, trapped in the body of some crippled person that can't do anything for herself!"

Lily erupted into a fit of sobs again, and when Morgan tried to comfort her, she pushed away fiercely. Morgan finally left the bathroom and called John. He came quickly, and he stayed with her for a long time. Finally, they emerged, John carrying her in his arms. She was sleeping soundly, lying against him.

"She'll be okay," John said, offering the best smile he could muster. Morgan took it, nodding her head. They stood there in the hallway for a moment before Morgan helped him out of the house, toting her wheelchair and folding it up to fit in the back of his car.

"I'll call tomorrow," Morgan said after John had closed the passenger door. He nodded and gave her a friendly wave before he settled inside and took off down the road.

The rain started outside shortly after. Morgan could hear it pattering against the roof of the house. She felt empty, hardly able to do anything except lie on the couch. It was getting late, but Morgan didn't think she could spend another second alone with her thoughts. Not ten minutes later, Abigail and Richard arrived, toting a piece of leftover cheesecake. Morgan brewed a pot of coffee, and the three sat in the living room together.

"She probably just needs some time," Abigail said, running her hand down Morgan's back. Morgan did her best to hold back the frustrated tears that were still falling down her face.

"You know," Richard said, as he stole a bite of the cheesecake they'd brought for Morgan. "I saw this documentary once about someone with amnesia. There was a husband who recreated old memories from their past."

"Honey, she doesn't need to hear about some documentary you saw-," Abigail shushed him. Richard had a fancy for watching documentaries and educational shows late at night before bed. It was always interesting what sort of random bit of information he'd bring up during conversation.

"That's what I tried to do with the lighthouse," Morgan argued. "I'm scared she's never going to get any of her memories back. And if she won't be able to walk on top of it—." She trailed off.

"Well," Richard said, and Morgan handed him the last bite of the dessert. "I think the guy from the documentary took her out on a date. Recreated the whole thing."

Morgan was about to protest when suddenly she had a thought. "I should take her to paint night."

"Take her to what?" Abigail asked, taking the plate away from her and walking it to the kitchen sink. Morgan could hear her rinsing it off when she got there.

"You don't need to do that," Morgan argued. "And paint night. The first date Lily and I ever went on. It was in Seattle, but I'm sure they have it here."

"They have some in Portland," Richard said, looking to Abigail. "Remember honey? Didn't you go with your friends the one time?"

Abigail snapped her fingers. "Oh, that was fun! I remember now. It was in a little café downtown."

Morgan's face lit up, and she felt a wave of optimism that she'd lacked most of the day. "I'll take her on a date."

The Beach

FROM THE MOMENT THAT Morgan Wallace met Lily Taylor on the beach in San Diego, she knew that their friendship was over. That it would never be the same again.

The sun was just starting to set, casting streaks of beautiful golden light across the waters. The sky was filled with shades of blues and purples and pink, blending together seamlessly into a tapestry of color. Morgan sat in the sand, watching the waves as they rolled in and out, crashing softly at the edges of her feet.

Lily had disappeared off down the beach somewhere to collect seashells. She'd always had a fascination for seashells, ever since she was a little kid. Morgan's mind drifted off while she waited for her. They'd been here four days now, enjoying the last remnants of their spring vacation before heading back to school.

Suddenly, over her shoulder there came a swift shout as she was attacked in a hug from behind. Admittedly, it had scared Morgan quite a bit, but it took her only a second to recover. She let out a laugh, her heart beating furiously in her chest. Lily came around to face the front of her, squatting down, so they met eyes.

"You're an easy scare," she laughed, ruffling the top of Morgan's hair. They stared at each other for a moment, Lily panting softly. Finally, just as she was about to get to her feet, Morgan wrapped her arms around Lily tightly and stood up. Lily squirmed in her grasp, giggling as Morgan trotted out into the ocean.

"No no no no no!"

Morgan leaped before Lily could do anything about it, and the two went tumbling into the waves. All the while, Morgan kept a careful grip on her. Lily squealed when they came up for air. "Oh, I hate you," she said loudly, all the while laughing.

"I hate you too," Morgan replied when she finally let her go. She looked at Lily then, dripping with salt water, the light from the sunset making her skin glow softly. That beautiful smile stretched across her face. It made Morgan's heart go into a frenzy. Just that small moment was all it took for Morgan to put twelve years of friendship on the line on a prayer that Lily might feel the same way.

Morgan moved towards her, their eyes not wavering. Lily's eyes watched her curiously. "Morgan," she breathed, and as she did, Morgan wrapped her arms around her waist and pulled her close. Then in one swift motion, she leaned in and pressed their lips firmly together. She could taste the salt water lingering on her and smelled it when she breathed her in. The air from Lily's nose tickled her skin. Neither of them pulled away. After a moment Morgan felt her kiss her back softly, and the gentle touch of her fingers against the side of her cheek.

It was over before it had even begun and when Lily finally left her, she stood with her fingers drawn up to her lips. Morgan thought she'd made the right decision until Lily's face turned horrified. Lily quickly turned and took off up the beach, towards a restaurant that sat out by the pier.

"Lily!" Morgan shouted after her, trying to keep up, but she was fast. As soon as Lily reached the restaurant, she disappeared into the bathroom, and Morgan was at her heel.

"I hate you," Lily said, her breath in slight pants. She rested her hand on the counter top, her back turned away. Morgan went to her, and as soon as she had, she placed a hand on her shoulder. "I really, really hate you."

"Lily," Morgan started, but she was quickly interrupted.

Lily turned towards her and pushed her back against the wall of the bathroom, and their lips met once more. Their bodies pressed together until there was no space between them and their mouths moved over one another's in a passionate fury. Morgan wrapped her hand around Lily's head, her fingers entangled in her damp wavy locks. Her heart beat furiously in her chest, nothing in the world able to tame it. She didn't care.

They stayed there until they had to breathe and when they pulled away, Morgan smiled.

"I hate you too," she whispered.

Chapter Four
Lily

THE NEXT MORNING, LILY found herself awake at six. She stared up at the ceiling for a while, exhausted from the lack of sleep. When she'd finally managed to wake up enough, she looked over at her wheelchair sitting at the foot of the bed. It was as if it was staring right back at her, taunting her. Lily hated it with every fiber of her being and wished desperately that she could will this whole nightmare away. Unable to stop herself, she cried, begging silently for her legs to move again. To be able to remember her life. For her body to not ache all the time.

When she'd finally recovered, she stared back at the wheelchair, realizing that unless she waited for her brother and sister-in-law to come get her, she'd be stuck in the bed. She took a deep breath, pushing herself into a sitting position. The sheets flung from her legs and she stared down at them, focusing with everything she had. Still, nothing changed. There was only the smallest of movements in her toes. She still couldn't feel her legs very much at all.

Lily cried again for a moment, but only a moment, before she wiped away her tears with the back of her hand. She stared over at the wheelchair for a long while, debating if she was brave enough.

Somehow, she managed to convince herself that she was and she reached out to roll it closer. After she'd gotten it situated, so it was against the nightstand and the side of the bed, she checked it to make sure it was steady. When she was satisfied, she pushed her body against the arm of the wheelchair and forced herself to scoot over to the edge of the bed. When her body was right where it needed to be, she took a deep breath and readied herself. Then, in one swift motion, she pushed herself up from the bed and fell into the seat of the wheelchair.

At first, it wobbled a bit, and Lily thought she might tip over. She had to adjust herself slightly, but she'd managed to get herself sitting upright and situated. After she moved each of her legs onto the foot-rests, she panted softly with a smile on her face. Lily hadn't felt this proud of anything for as long as she could remember. She sat there for a moment, basking in her accomplishment before she rolled her way to the door and let herself out of the room.

The house was quiet. Lily did her best to keep it that way as she worked her way down the hallway. At first, she found it hard to move, the wheels turning on her every couple of feet so she'd have to adjust herself as to not hit the wall. When she finally made it into the living room, another wave of happiness overcame her.

Lily sat for a moment catching her breath. As she did, a picture caught her eye on the mantle of the fireplace. She rolled closer, reaching up carefully to pull it from its resting place. It was a picture of Morgan and her, standing in front of the lighthouse. Morgan had her arm wrapped around her waist, and Lily was kissing her softly on the cheek. They both looked so happy. Lily wondered if it was from when they'd first moved into the lighthouse together. As she placed it back, she noticed another picture beside it. This time it was a familiar one, and it took her breath away.

Lily had been a sophomore in high school, John a junior in college. It was two days before Christmas. They had taken a family photo every year since John had been born. Lily remembered this instance specifically because it had been the first year she could recall not wanting to take the picture. She'd been late for a date, and the last thing she wanted to do was waste an hour while her father played with every setting on his camera.

If only she had known better.

Three days after Christmas there had been a small snowstorm. Lily's father had always been notoriously bad with preparing ahead of time, so he and her mother had gone out to the store to fetch some food in the midst of it. John had been watching television and Lily reading a book when the doorbell had rung.

The snowplow had hit a large patch of black ice and skidded two hundred feet downhill. When it had collided with their parent's car, it had flipped, sending them all down off the side of a road into a ditch. Neither of their parents had made it to the hospital. Lily couldn't remember much more of that night after the police had shown up at her house. Only that she couldn't sleep alone for months. Morgan had spent nearly every day at her house after that night, and John barely let her from his sight until she'd gone off to college.

Lily found it hard to breathe for a moment as her fingers grazed over the frame. Just as she placed the photo back on the mantle, she felt a hand on her shoulder.

"Did you get out of bed all by yourself?" John asked her, a hint of surprise in his voice. Lily looked up at him with a small smile on her face and nodded. He looked genuinely impressed for a moment before his face grew concerned. "You should really be careful."

For a moment Lily felt frustrated. "I can handle myself just fine John. You don't always have to take care of me."

John looked as if he might respond for a moment but then chose not to. The two of them sat and stared at the pictures on the mantle for a while until he finally looked back down at her.

"Would you like to go see them today?" John nodded to the picture. Lily didn't even have to respond, and he knew the answer.

After Elise made breakfast and Lily had filled herself up with coffee, she and John made their way over to the cemetery a few miles down the road. Their father had always loved Maple trees. John had found the perfect plot underneath two that sat side by side. When they'd buried them, they'd been barren and empty, but now they were full of beautiful green leaves. John helped her navigate through the row until they'd reached their gravestones.

John sat beside her, and they were silent for a long while, enjoying the soft winds blowing and the scent of the morning air. Suddenly Lily felt something fall into her lap.

"I thought you could read it this time," John said.

Every time they came to visit, the two of them would read a poem from her father's favorite anthology. It had been a tradition of sorts. Lily flipped through the pages till she happened on her favorite one. EE Cummings.

"maggie and milly and molly and may

went down to the beach(to play one day)

and maggie discovered a shell that sang

so sweetly she couldn't remember her troubles,and

milly befriended a stranded star

whose rays five languid fingers were;

and molly was chased by a horrible thing

which raced sideways while blowing bubbles:and

may came home with a smooth round stone

as small as a world and as large as alone."

Before she finished, her hands swept over the page, staring at the last line.

"For whatever we lose(like a you or a me)

it's always ourselves we find in the sea."

Lily felt herself crying when she read it, tears spilling into the pages. John placed a hand on her back and let her, without speaking.

When they'd gotten back to the house, Lily was in a solemn mood. Surprisingly, it wasn't entirely because of her parents. Instead, she thought about Morgan and the incident the night before. Elise did her best to distract her most of the late morning by having her help finish decorating the nursery. After Lily had hung pictures and folded sheets into a drawer, she started to feel more optimistic, in spite of her circumstances.

A little after lunch, there was a knock at the door. When John answered, she could hear Morgan outside. Lily started to head down the hallway in an attempt to hide when John peeked his head around the door to call out after her.

"Morgan's here to see you," he said, and Lily wheeled herself back around. She and John exchanged a silent glance before she finally nodded her head.

John turned back towards Morgan and waved her inside. When she appeared from behind the door, she was carrying a bouquet of lilies. Lily couldn't help but smile, in spite of herself.

"I just came over to say sorry for last night," Morgan said as she approached her. When she handed over the flowers, Lily breathed them in for a moment. They were still slightly damp from being watered. "And to ask you a question."

Lily looked up at her curiously and watched as Morgan took in a deep breath.

"I was wondering if I could take you out on a date," she said, and they exchanged a look before she continued. "No strings attached, no expectations. I just wanted to take you out tonight, if you'd be interested."

Lily pondered on the idea for a moment, not sure what to say in response. Finally, she decided to nod, and she looked back up at her. "Okay."

The look on Morgan's face was priceless. "Really?" Lily nodded again, and her smile only proceeded to get bigger. "Great! I'll pick you up at six."

"Where are we going?" Lily asked her as Morgan turned to leave.

"It's a surprise," Morgan said with a mischievous looking smile. "But I'm pretty sure you're going to like it."

Lily's stomach was in knots the entire afternoon. John and Elise did their best to distract her with more chores. After they'd finished, John went down to the basement to fetch something.

When he returned, John had found a box of Lily's and handed it to her. It read "PROPERTY OF LILY TAYLOR ONLY!" On another side: "NO TOUCHING! THIS MEANS YOU, JOHN!" Lily laughed when she read it and looked up to her brother, who shrugged.

"You're pretty feisty, I figured I should listen," John said, rooting through another box beside her. Lily smiled at him before she opened the one in her lap. Inside lay mementos from her childhood. Things she hadn't seen in a decade.

"Remember this?" Lily asked as she pulled out a string of postcards from their summer trip across the states. When John looked over, he smiled. One summer break when they were younger, their parents had surprised them with a trip down the coast. They'd stopped in every state, all the way to Florida. Lily could still remember the white sandy beaches. She'd collected seashells from every place they'd stopped at. She rooted through the box and found them in a jar buried under some papers.

When she moved it, she noticed a folded up envelope with Morgan's handwriting scribbled on the outside. "Happy Valentine's Day." It read on the outside. When she opened it, there was an old CD inside.

"What's this?" Lily asked John, and he shrugged. As she sat it in her lap, Elise peeked her head into the room. "Can I steal you for a bit?" When Lily looked at the clock, she realized it was already a little after five.

Elise took her to their bedroom and rooted through clothes to find a nice looking dress. "You'll look perfect in this," she assured Lily as the two of them worked together to get her out of her sweats and t-shirt. Once she'd gotten situated, Elise did a lap around her looking pleased with herself. "Will you let me fix your hair?"

Lily hadn't had someone pamper her since her mother had been alive. It sent a wave of memories through her that she had to fight to hold back. She smiled and nodded, and Elise set to work. She gave her hair a little bit of a curl, and Lily let her fix her makeup. Lily had insisted not to go too overboard as to give Morgan the wrong idea about the whole affair. She still hadn't quite recovered from the previous night's events.

Promptly at six, Morgan arrived. When John answered the door, Lily sat behind him. The two met eyes and Lily felt her heart do a little jump in her chest. She wasn't the only one who had gone through the trouble of looking nice. Morgan had tamed her head of thick curls and, like

Lily had picked out a dress to wear. Lily couldn't remember the last time she'd seen her in one.

"You look really nice," Morgan said, in a casual way. "Are you ready?" Lily nodded, and John wheeled her out to the car. Just as he was about to lift her inside, Lily stopped him.

"Let me try to do it," she said.

John looked hesitant. "I don't think that's a good idea." He started to help her and Lily pushed him away.

"John," she said, looking back up to him sternly. "I want to try to do it." John took a step back, and as he did, Lily pulled both of her legs into the car, one by one. Then she hoisted herself up as best she could, grasping a hold of the car door. She swung her body towards the inside of the car and found herself tumbling softly inside.

Both Morgan and John rushed to her aid, and all Lily could find herself doing was laughing. As they came to help her, she batted them away, sitting herself up as best she could. Lily was in pants after the fact, and her body ached, but she felt satisfied.

John leaned inside the car giving her a worried look before he planted a kiss on her cheek. "Have a good time," he said, squeezing her shoulder before he exited and shut the door behind him.

A minute later Morgan joined her in the car, looking genuinely impressed. "John said you got in your wheelchair all by yourself this morning?" Lily paused for a second but then nodded. "That's amazing." Lily couldn't help but smile a little.

"So where are we going?" She asked as Morgan backed out of the driveway.

"I told you," Morgan replied. "It's a surprise. You're going to have to wait and see." Lily was about to protest but stopped herself. They enjoyed the car ride, mostly keeping to themselves while Morgan drove. When she was tired of the silence, Lily dug through her purse and pulled out the CD that she had found earlier.

"What's this?" Lily asked Morgan, holding up the CD. "I don't remember it."

"It looks like a CD to me," Morgan joked, giving her a smile.

"I found it in an old box of mine this afternoon. It was from you."

Morgan snatched the CD from her and popped it into the player. "I guess we'll just have to find out."

When the music started to play, Lily sat for a while trying to place the instrument she was hearing. It sounded somewhat like a guitar. Before she could decide, she heard Morgan's voice echo through the car singing "You Are My Sunshine." Lily looked up at her and smiled.

"Since when do you play the ukulele?" she asked as she finally realized what it was. "And I didn't know you could sing."

"I bought it our trip to San Diego junior year. It was a surprise. I think we were slightly drunk," Morgan smiled. "You wanted me to play songs for you, so I learned 'You Are My Sunshine' in the hotel that night." She laughed. "And sing badly, you mean."

Lily smiled, listening to her in the background. "Do you still play?"

"A little," Morgan admitted. "Not so much since we moved to the lighthouse."

There it was again. All those memories Lily didn't have. Instead of dwelling on it, Lily turned to her and smiled softly. "Tell me about when we first moved in."

Morgan told her the story, back from when they had first found out about Patrick Wallace passing away, up to the point where they were drowning in so many boxes at their new house that they didn't know where to put everything. By the time the two pulled into the parking lot of an old café in downtown Portland, they both were nearly in tears laughing at Morgan's memories of their catastrophe of a move.

As the car parked, Lily's mind suddenly became filled with dread. As Morgan went to get her wheelchair from the back, she watched as a couple walked hand-in-hand into the restaurant. Another family followed shortly after, walking up the steps to the entrance. At that moment, all Lily could think about was how she wouldn't be walking inside. She was entirely dependent on Morgan. As much as she appreciated the help, the thought filled her with sadness she could not soothe. Morgan parked the wheelchair next to the passenger side door and opened it. Afterward, she scooped Lily into her arms and set her down gently.

The two shared a glance for a moment. It must have been obvious that something was wrong, because Morgan could tell almost instantly. "What's the matter?"

Lily shook her head, trying to fight the thoughts. They took off towards the entrance. When they reached the edge of the curb of the road, Morgan tilted her up and cleared it with ease.

"I think I'm going to have to carry you up the stairs," Morgan realized, and Lily felt every part of her start to sink deep into the wheelchair, utterly humiliated. Before Morgan could reach down to grasp hold of her, Lily placed a hand on her wrist.

"I can't," she breathed, holding back a stifled cry.

Morgan looked at her curiously, walking around to stand in front of her. "What do you mean?"

"I don't think I can do this. Not yet." Lily said. Another couple approached, staring at her as tears started to fall down her face. "Can we go back to the car?" she begged in a whisper, and immediately Morgan turned the wheelchair around and went straight back.

As soon as they both had made it inside, Lily took a long deep breath, fighting back her tears. "I'm sorry, Morgan," she managed to say, wiping her face with her hands. Lily wondered for a moment if she might pry into why she'd refused, but instead, Morgan started the car and smiled.

"That's why you always have a backup plan," she said, giving Lily a wink.

The two drove down the street to the convenience store where Morgan disappeared for a few minutes. Lily stared out down the city streets, the sun disappearing. As she started to drift off into her thoughts, Morgan returned bearing bags of goodies. While she pulled out of the parking lot, Lily rooted through them.

"Did you buy enough snacks?" she laughed. "Oh! You got me chocolate!"

Morgan waved her hand at her while she turned out onto the main stretch of road. "Save it for a few more minutes." Lily looked at her curiously but did as she was told. As promised, it only took a few minutes to make their way across town. Just as Lily was about to ask where they were going again, Morgan pulled off the road down the long paved street of the Portland Drive-In. The last time the two of them had been here was back in grade school when her parents had taken them on the weekends.

"I can't believe this place is still open!" Lily exclaimed as Morgan got their tickets.

They barely watched the movie, too engrossed in conversation and stuffing their faces with all the junk food they could eat. It wasn't until they'd noticed most of the cars had left that they figured out the movie had ended.

Lily looked down at the empty bag of chocolates she had devoured entirely on her own. "I'm going to feel that tomorrow," she moaned, cradling her stomach.

Morgan laughed and smiled at her. Lily watched as Morgan leaned over and gently rubbed the side of her mouth with her thumb. "It's all over your face." As Morgan drew her hand over her cheek, Lily found she rather enjoyed the feeling. Her face nuzzled into Morgan's hand just for a moment. The two of the met eyes when she did, and they stared deeply at one another. Morgan's hand didn't move away, and Lily didn't want it to.

Suddenly the two of them drew closer together. Time seemed to stand still at that moment as they moved effortlessly. Lily felt Morgan's other hand wrap onto her face and watched her big green eyes as they pierced into her. Her body moved towards Morgan, pulled by such a strong force that she wasn't able to stop herself. Just as their mouths were about to meet, Lily placed a hand on Morgan's chest and took a breath in through her nose.

Lily stared at her, their faces barely separated before she quickly pulled away. "Did you just fart?" She sniffed the air, her face twisting into a look of disgust.

Morgan looked mortified, her face going bright red. "It was an accident!"

"Oh my God, Morgan!" Lily laughed as she rolled down the window, wafting the smell from the car.

There was a silent air as Morgan drove back down the road towards Kennebunkport. Lily caught careful glances of her, wondering what she was thinking. Finally, she cleared her throat, deciding to break the silence. "What was the original date you had planned?" They exchanged quick glances, and Lily watched a smile spread across Morgan's face.

"I was going to take you to paint night," she admitted.

"Our first date?" Lily asked, and Morgan nodded. Suddenly she felt horribly guilty for having ruined the idea. "I'm sorry." Lily's hand wrapped around Morgan's hand that was laying on the armrest next to her. She didn't let it go until they'd pulled into the driveway at John's. By then Lily had started to doze.

Morgan unloaded her from the car, wrapping Lily carefully in her arms. Lily looked up at her as she carried her inside. John offered to take her, but Morgan declined, making her way down the hall to the guest room where Lily was staying. After the door was shut, they worked together to get Lily changed into pajamas. Morgan let her do as much of it as she could handle and let her climb into bed on her own. Lily could hear the wind rattling the windows slightly as Morgan threw the sheets over her and sat down on the edge of the bed. The two met eyes and Lily broke into a soft smile. "I had a really nice time tonight."

"Me too," Morgan returned her smile. They stared at each other for a moment before Lily felt herself reach up and tug at Morgan's shirt, drawing her downward. It happened in one perfect moment, their lips meeting. Lily took a deep breath in, kissing her briefly before she loosened her grip and Morgan sat back up. She could feel her cheeks getting hot realizing what she had done.

"Goodnight, Lily," Morgan said, situating her covers for a moment.

"Goodnight, Morgan," Lily replied as she watched her make her way from the room. When she'd closed the door behind her, Lily brought her fingers to her lips, sighing softly.

The Ukulele

THE FIRST TIME THAT Lily Taylor realized she was in love with Morgan Wallace was in a hotel room in San Diego, being serenaded by the worlds most out of tune ukulele.

"Come on, Morgan," Lily had begged her as they walked past the music store window, both of them having had a glass of wine too much at dinner. "Don't you want to sing me a song with your wonderful sweet voice?" Lily stared up at the instruments hanging from the display.

"I don't sing," Morgan argued, tugging at her arm a bit. Lily laughed, and the two wandered down the street back to the hotel.

While Lily took a bath, Morgan called to her from the door. "I'm going to go downstairs for a minute. I'll be right back." Lily thought nothing of it, finishing her bath and wrapping herself in a robe afterward. When she opened the bathroom door, she could hear the off-pitch plucks of a familiar instrument.

Lily turned the corner, surprised to find Morgan stretched out on the bed, her phone playing chords from a video while a ukulele was sitting in her lap.

"You went back to the music store?" Lily stared at her in disbelief. Morgan looked up and smiled, strumming the instrument quietly.

The two sat side by side on the bed, Lily with her head on Morgan's shoulder as she learned the chords. All the while, Lily watched her curiously. It took an hour but eventually, Morgan cleared her throat, and Lily sat up to look at her.

"Alright, are you ready?" Morgan asked, shaking her head in embarrassment. "I'm only doing this once."

Lily laughed and sat upright, so she was facing her.

"*You are my sunshine, my only sunshine..*" Morgan sang in a terribly adorable off-key voice, strumming along the equally out-of-tune chords. "*You make me happy when skies are grey.*"

Lily sang along with her at the end, "*You'll never know dear, how much I love you.*" When she sang it, the two looked up to one another, Morgan's big green eyes staring deeply at her. "*Please don't take my sunshine away.*"

As Morgan strummed the last chord, she looked back down at the instrument, running her fingers over the strings.

"That probably wasn't what you were expecting," Morgan started, looking rather embarrassed.

Lily moved her body towards her, taking the ukulele from her hands and setting it on the bed behind her.

"I probably could sing it better with a little more practice," Morgan continued to ramble. Lily inched closer, till there was hardly any space between them. When Morgan finally looked up at her, their faces were barely apart.

"Morgan," Lily said softly, running her hand along the side of Morgan's face.

"Mm," she replied, their eyes not wavering.

"I love you," Lily smiled, letting their noses touch. Morgan let out the deepest happiest sigh she'd ever heard before their lips and bodies came together seamlessly.

Chapter Five
Morgan

WHEN MORGAN RETURNED to the lighthouse, the sky was full of stars, stretching in every direction. In spite of the fact that she'd woken early, she didn't feel much like sleeping. Instead, she fetched herself a beer and walked down the path to the docks. She sat on the edge, sliding her feet into the water. It felt nice, soothing even. The ripples cascaded in every direction as she swept her feet around in a circle.

After she took a drink, Morgan laid her body back against the dock, staring up into the night. Every few seconds the lighthouse beacon would cast a glow over the skies as it passed by. It was almost hypnotic in a way.

Morgan thought of Lily then and the kiss they'd shared what felt like only moments earlier. She could still feel it faintly lingering on her lips. There wasn't a time in recent memory she'd felt so happy and content, realizing that there was still a chance to have her back.

In the distance, Morgan heard a call. When sat up and turned her head, she saw a faint figure walking down the pathway where she'd just come from. It only took her a second to realize it was Abigail. She waved as she approached and Morgan waved back to her quietly.

"I saw you walking down here, I wanted to make sure you were alright." Abigail gave her a smile as she walked down the docks to meet her.

"I'm fine," Morgan replied, smiling back. "I just got back from John's."

"How did your date go?" Abigail asked as she sat beside her, dipping her feet in the water. Morgan sighed softly, still smiling. She felt her friends glance on the side of her face before she gently shoved her.

"That good, huh?" Abigail replied, kicking at the water with her foot.

Morgan proceeded to reiterate the night's events while Abigail listened. When she told her about the kiss, Abigail's smile got bigger than Morgan had seen it in years. "Really? Sweetheart, that's wonderful!" Her hand ran across Morgan's back, rubbing it softly. "See? Everything is going to be okay, you just have to be patient." Morgan nodded, looking back out at the water.

"Well, I'm going to go. Richard was about ready for bed. He had some documentary going when I left him." Abigail said finally, getting to her feet. "I just wanted to check on you. You two should come to the bakery sometime."

Morgan nodded at the idea. "Thanks," she replied, looking up and smiling at her. A moment later Abigail disappeared down the dock and made her way back up the hill. Turning towards the water, Morgan laid herself down on the dock again and proceeded to get lost in her thoughts for a brief while before she picked herself up and made her way back to the lighthouse.

The next morning, Morgan woke at six to start her chores as usual. Once she'd finished, she fixed herself some coffee and fried some eggs and bacon on the stovetop. As she was sitting down to eat, the lights began to flicker in the kitchen. Morgan looked up at them, starting to feel an anger boil inside of her. Memories of that night a few weeks prior came flooding back to her. She slammed her hand against the wall in rapid succession and cursed. It did nothing.

"This ends today," she said aloud, to no one in particular.

After she'd cleaned up breakfast and put a sign up at the museum explaining she was out for the morning, Morgan searched on her laptop for various fixes to the electrical problems she'd been having. Once she found some instructions, she made a list of parts she needed and headed into town. The hardware store was opening when she arrived. She spent most of the morning finding the things she needed and running a few extra errands before she made her way back.

Just as Morgan was pulling into the driveway, she saw John's car parked near the house. By the time Morgan had gotten out of her car, John had rolled Lily up, giving a wave.

"What are you doing here?" Morgan asked curiously. When Lily and she met eyes, it was only for a minute before Lily looked away blushing. Morgan turned her attention back to John momentarily.

"Lily wanted to come over, so I told her I'd take her on my lunch break," John said. "I tried calling you but you didn't pick up, so I thought we'd drop by."

Morgan glanced at her phone and realized she'd had missed calls. She must have been so distracted in the hardware store she hadn't paid attention.

"I'm not doing much today," Morgan said, looking down to Lily. "I was going to make some repairs." She raised the bags of supplies in her hands.

"Can I help?" Lily asked her. She looked genuinely excited about the idea.

"Lily," John placed a hand on her shoulder. "I don't think you need to over-extend yourself yet." Lily waved him off, looking back to Morgan.

"I guess if you really want to," Morgan said, scratching the back of her head. Lily looked pleased and took the bags from her hands.

"Take care of her," John said, still looking concerned. Morgan gave him a nod before he hopped back in his car and took off down the road.

"You're the first person in the history of man that I've seen so excited about doing house repairs." Morgan picked her up from the wheelchair and carried her up the steps inside. After she sat her down on the couch. Lily watched her as she retrieved a toolbox and then sat down beside her on the couch with her laptop. The two watched the videos Morgan had found on the repairs they needed to do.

"So the first thing we're going to do is replace all the light fixtures in here. I think that's the reason why the lights are flickering. They're just old." Morgan loaded Lily into the wheelchair and sat the toolbox in her lap. The two made their way over to the first fixture hanging above the entryway to the house. Morgan opened all the blinds in the living room and walked down to turn off the breaker that controlled the power.

"Can you hand me a Philips' head?" Morgan asked as she stepped onto the ladder. Lily dug through the toolbox and handed it to her. Afterward, Morgan stepped onto the stool and carefully unscrewed the fixture from the ceiling. Once she had, she tossed it onto the couch while Lily unboxed the new fixture. Morgan made sure all the screws on the electrical box were tightened before she fastened it to the ceiling. When she'd replaced the lightbulbs, she stepped off the ladder and clapped her hands together. "A few more," she smiled at Lily, and they moved to the next one.

The whole ordeal took about an hour before Morgan was satisfied. Afterwards, she went back to the breaker to turn back on the power. As soon as she had, she heard Lily cheering on the other end of the house. Morgan was pleased when she came back into the living room.

"They look really nice," Lily said, admiring their work. "They go well with everything."

"Next time I'm bringing you to help me," Morgan replied, giving her a smile. "You're the one who is always good at picking out that sort of thing."

"I don't know," Lily shrugged. "You did a good job." Morgan's smile didn't leave her face. She came back to sit on the couch again, and Lily moved on her own to sit beside her. They watched another video on how to check the wiring behind the light switches and spent another few hours checking all the ones throughout the house. When they finally finished, Morgan felt satisfied that the flickering light days were behind her.

It was nearing dinner. Morgan fried up some chicken and vegetables, and they sat at the kitchen table in silence, enjoying their food. Finally Lily looked up at her, offering a smile.

"Can I ask you a question? It's kind of personal?" She took a bite of chicken as Morgan looked up to meet her glance. "I was wondering. You said that you were planning on eventually letting volunteers run the lighthouse and we'd move closer to Portland. Can I ask you why you want to give up the lighthouse? It's just.. it's been your dream ever since I can remember. To live here."

Morgan stared at her for a long while in disbelief. It took her a moment to bring herself back to the reality that this was a new Lily. The fight from the boat replayed in her mind like a nightmare she wanted so desperately to forget. Eventually, she forced a smile, doing her best to come up with the most logical explanation.

"I wanted to come work with you," Morgan finally decided to say. She could tell the minute she said it that Lily wasn't satisfied with the an-

swer. Yet she didn't press her, only nodded and finished off the last bite
of her food.

"It wasn't because of me, was it?" Lily asked her finally as Morgan went
to pick up their plates. "The reason why you'd give this place up? You
said I didn't like it here."

"It wasn't because of you," Morgan assured her, washing the dishes in
the sink. She let her hands run under the warm water, enjoying the
relaxing feeling. Lily came up beside her, and Morgan handed off the
plates so she could dry them with a tea towel. After they finished, Morgan rolled her neck and shoulders, both aching from working on the
ceiling half the afternoon. Lily took notice and tugged at her wrist.

Morgan sat on the floor while Lily sat on the couch, the two of them
watching the news that played mindlessly in the background. After
she'd pulled her hair up, Morgan relaxed as Lily's hands worked over
her shoulders and neck. It had been a long time since she'd given a mas-
sage, but it was as good as Morgan remembered it being. While she
worked, the two chatted about memories of their school days. Eventually, Lily's arms draped around Morgan's shoulders, and she nudged
their heads together.

"Feel better?" She asked, and Morgan nodded, tilting her head back
to look up at Lily. They stared at each other for a moment quietly.
Lily softly ran her fingers through Morgan's curls, letting her fingertips
stroke the top of her head. Morgan found herself sighing at the feeling,
closing her eyes for a moment. Lily leaned down and gently kissed her
upside-down, letting their lips run together briefly.

Just as Morgan turned to face her, the doorbell rang through the house,
causing the two of them to jump. Morgan looked at the clock and realized it was going on after six.

"I bet you money that's your brother," Morgan said, aggravated. Sure enough, when she went to answer the door, he was standing outside, hands in his pockets. The two of them walked up the stairs together, and Morgan could tell when she looked at Lily she was still trying to recover.

"Are you ready?" John asked, and Lily nodded. While he carried her out to the car, Morgan toted the wheelchair. After she'd loaded it inside, she came around to the passenger seat to look at Lily for a moment. When they met eyes, they both smiled. Morgan leaned in and gently kissed her on the cheek goodbye and watched as Lily blushed. They said their goodnights and John gave Morgan a wave before the two took off down the road.

The following afternoon, after Morgan had finished chores and had given an early morning tour, she got a phone call from a number she'd been avoiding for at least a month. As much as she tried to convince herself to not answer, she found herself doing so anyway.

"Mom?" Morgan asked as she put the phone to her ear. Instead, she was surprised to hear her father's gruff cough in the background. When he spoke, he sounded as if he'd already gotten started on his drinks a little too early. Morgan sat down on the couch, wrapping her hand around her forehead.

"Morgan," he said firmly. "You need to come over." Morgan sighed into the phone, feeling her body tense just at the idea of it.

"What's going on, Dad?" She asked, sitting back on the couch. In all actuality, she wanted nothing to do with it, but he was going to tell her regardless.

"Your mother won't get out of bed," he replied, coughing again. "I've tried to make her get up all morning. I called the office and everything. This is the fifth time this month she's skipped work."

"Can you put her on the phone?" Morgan asked him.

"She won't talk to anyone," her father replied. "All she does is just lie in the damn bed all day. You need to come over."

"I'll be over in a bit," Morgan sighed, hanging up the phone. She sat on the couch for a while, taking deep breaths and trying to convince herself that she could handle the situation. If Lily had been around, she would have likely gone with her. Today, however, she'd have to go alone. Anxiety washed over her at a rapid pace, but Morgan managed to force her way through it.

An hour later, Morgan took the winding roads to the far north of Kennebunkport, to her parent's old cottage home at the end of a dead-end street. She parked the car in the driveway and was surprised when her father Paul opened the door even before she had reached it. For the first time in a long while, Morgan saw genuine concern in his eyes when they looked at one another.

"I think she's depressed," he said as Morgan made her way inside. "She comes home from work and goes straight to bed, and she's missed so many days this month they're threatening to fire her."

Morgan's mother Mary had worked for the post office for nearly thirty years. She was set to retire in another five and had always loved her job.

Before she turned into the hallway to the bedroom, Morgan noticed the beer bottle on the end table on the couch. "How many beers have you had today, Dad?" Paul scoffed at her as they stood there for a moment.

"Yes, I had one. Now mind your damn business and go check on your mother, please."

At least he had said please because if he hadn't Morgan felt she would have likely snapped at him. Instead, she turned and wandered down the hallway and landed a swift knock on the bedroom door.

"Mom?" she asked softly as she started to open the door. "Can I come in?" When there was no answer, Morgan swung the door open the rest of the way. Its knob was loose and barely hanging on, much like everything else in their old rickety house. Mary was lying curled up on the edge of the bed, looking miserable.

"Morgan?" Her mother said meekly as Morgan moved to the edge of the bed and sat beside her. She put a soft hand on Mary's shoulder and rubbed it gently.

"What's going on, Mom?" Morgan asked her. "Dad says you've been missing work."

Mary sighed and rolled over on her back, looking up at the ceiling. "I don't know what's wrong with me. I can't get out of bed in the morning."

"Do you want to go talk to someone?"

"Those shrinks don't know what they're talking about," Morgan's mother sighed, looking up to her. "They always tell me I'm depressed and I need medication or this that and the other."

"What if you are depressed, Mom? Wouldn't you want help?" It hadn't been a minute or two into the conversation, and Morgan could already feel herself getting frustrated. She forced it down, focusing on doing her best to stay positive for her mom. As she situated herself, she got a whiff of her mother, who too seemed like she'd been drinking. "What does Dad say?"

"Your father wants me to go to work," she moaned. "He doesn't understand that I *can't* go."

"Let's get you an appointment," Morgan begged her. "I'll even go with you if you want. Dad and I both. Would that help?"

Morgan's mother sighed and rolled away from her again. "I'm fine Morgan. I can handle it on my own."

"Clearly you can't—" Morgan started, but she was quickly interrupted by her mother pulling herself up from the bed. Once she'd gotten to her feet, she wiped her face with the back of her hands and took a deep breath in.

"I'm fine, Morgan. Now, do you want to stay for dinner? I was thinking about making a roast."

Morgan stared at her for a long time, not speaking. Baffled at the fact that she'd just dismissed her. "I'm okay Mom, I have things I need to take care of at home." Her mother looked a little saddened but nodded anyway. "How about I take you out for breakfast next week? Before work? Would that be okay?" It seemed to cheer Mary up a little when she asked.

Before she decided to take her leave, Morgan pulled her father outside onto the porch. He reeked of alcohol and Morgan was quite sure he'd had started on another drink while she'd been in the room with her mother.

"You need to try to take her to see a counselor," Morgan told him flatly. "She needs someone to talk to and to get her some medications or something to help her feel better."

Paul stared at her for a moment before he responded. "Don't you think I have suggested that to her before? She doesn't listen."

"Dad," Morgan sighed, frustrated. "You're going to *have* to make her listen. This isn't a negotiation. She's depressed. Clearly, you see that. This can't keep happening."

On cue, her father said the thing she had predicted he'd argue from the beginning. "You know those shrinks are expensive. It's not like we have a bunch of money floating around."

"I'll pay for it if I have to," Morgan argued. "Just please get her to go. I'm serious."

"I'll try," Paul said, shrugging. "But I'm not promising anything."

That was the last thing Morgan could take. She took a step off the porch and turned back towards him. "Have a good night, Dad." It was a habitual thing to say, nothing more. The only thing she really felt was anger towards the whole situation, but she managed to hold it down.

Once she'd gotten back into the car and her father disappeared back inside the house, Morgan slammed her hands into the steering wheel, crying. Every time she promised herself she wouldn't get in the middle of their problems. Yet, every time she found herself at their aid again. Morgan knew her father wouldn't do a damn thing to help her mother, even though she'd begged him to. Mary wouldn't do anything to help herself either, not without being forced. Once again, that responsibility fell on her shoulders, as much as she didn't want it to.

They'd go out to breakfast next week. Somehow, Morgan would convince her mother that she needed to go to therapy. That was all there was to it.

Morgan didn't see Lily again until the end of the week. The lighthouse suddenly grew full of visitors, and Lily wanted to spend time with her brother. It wasn't until Friday afternoon that Morgan finally called and asked her if she'd like to go on another date. Lily, who was surprisingly good at freaking Morgan out, immediately told her no.

"Okay," Morgan said, taken slightly aback. The line grew silent for a moment before Lily let out a little laugh and Morgan felt her heart settle back into her chest. "I hate you," she said, laughing along with Lily.

They agreed for Morgan to come to the house at seven and just before she went to hang up the phone, Lily caught her.

"Hey Morgan," Lily said, in a curious tone of voice. "Can I stay the night tonight?"

Morgan felt her heart do flips in her chest. It had been over a week since Lily had last stayed at the lighthouse. Every night she missed her, to the point that she had started using pillows to pretend she had someone beside her. It wasn't even remotely the same.

"Of course," Morgan said quickly, and she could swear Lily was smiling on the other end of the line.

"See you at seven."

Right on time, Morgan sat out in the driveway of John's house taking a few deep breaths before she went to pick Lily up. As she got out of the car, Lily was rolling down the sidewalk in her wheelchair on her own. She looked beautiful, her hair pulled up behind her head, wearing a cute blouse. She looked even more spectacular tonight than she had on their first date, as crazy as that was to think. But Morgan didn't believe there had ever been a day that Lily hadn't looked nice.

"I wanted to go for a walk," Lily said and then for a brief moment looked slightly sad. "I mean, I wanted to get out of the house for a little while." She shook the thought away, looking to Morgan.

"How do you feel about dessert before dinner?" Morgan asked, changing the subject. Lily looked at her curiously as she pulled herself into the car.

The two made it across town to Abigail and Richard's bakery. While she was often treated to leftovers, it had been a while since she'd actually been there. So long in fact, that there had been new renovations. It was getting close to closing time for the store, so Morgan did her best to hurry and walk Lily inside.

Abigail was waiting at the counter when they arrived and smiled happily. "Oh, you came by!" She clapped her hands, looking at Lily. "How are you feeling?"

"Good," Lily said, looking at her.

"Oh right, I'm sorry." Abigail made her way over to Lily, sticking out her hand. "I'm Abigail. We live next door to the lighthouse."

Lily's smiled then, nodding. "Morgan's told me a lot about you."

"Come in, come in," Abigail waved and ushered them to a table. "Richard! The girls are here!" A moment later, Richard came out from the kitchen, covered in flour and various other ingredients. He wiped his head with the back of his hand and smiled.

"It's about time you came back to visit," he said, pulling up a chair next to Morgan.

The four of them chatted for a while, and Morgan was pleased to find that Lily got along with them as well now as she had before the accident. Before long, it was as if they were old friends, joking with each other and relaxed.

When they were getting ready to leave for the evening, Richard bundled up some macaroons for them to take home. After Lily and Morgan had gotten back into the car, the two looked at each other smiling.

"They are really nice," Lily said, looking down into the bag of macaroons. "I'm glad they're our neighbors."

It was a subtle thing, and Lily hadn't seemed to catch it, but Morgan did. The way she had said *our* made her heart flutter with even more hope than it already had.

By the time they had gotten back to the lighthouse, Lily had devoured the entire bag of macaroons.

"Sorry," she said, her face covered in guilt. "I saved you one at least."

"You can have it," Morgan smiled as she started to get out of the car. "So long as you eat my dinner. I'm making salmon."

"My favorite!" Lily sighed, smiling as Morgan disappeared around the car to fetch her. After she'd wrapped Lily in her arms, Morgan made her way up the steps into the house, setting her down at the kitchen table. Lily finished off the last macaroon, just as Morgan went to put her prepared food from the fridge into the oven. She poured them each a glass of wine and sat at the table across from her.

"So," Morgan said, clearing her throat. "The first night we moved in, we had a night picnic out on the docks. It was your idea. Every month after, on the first Friday, we'd go out and have another picnic together. It's kind of our thing."

Lily looked at her curiously. "So it's supposed to be tonight?" Morgan nodded, and Lily looked genuinely excited. She took a sip of wine, and Morgan noticed that she couldn't stop smiling.

"What?" Morgan asked, and Lily shook her head, waving her off. When she looked away, Morgan watched her eyes as they drifted to the ukulele sitting in the seat beside her.

"Were you playing without me?" Lily asked, reaching for it. She set it in her lap, strumming it softly. It still sounded off-key, but much better than Morgan ever remembered it sounding. "Is this the one from college?"

Morgan took it from her and began to tune it a bit. "I was just playing around with it earlier."

"Play me a song," Lily said, smiling at her.

"I'm not that good," Morgan admitted as she finished fixing the strings well enough. Her hands strummed over them again. "There was this song I wanted to play for you though if you wanted to hear it. I wrote it for you last year. You hadn't heard it yet."

Lily looked genuinely surprised. "Now you *have* to play it."

Morgan felt her face get hot thinking about the idea of playing for her. It had been so long since she had. She took another big swallow of wine and cleared her a throat. A few chords were strummed and then she started to sing.

"Lily," Morgan sang, strumming a chord.

"Can't you see what you do to me?

Every smile you make runs through me.

Every word you speak seems to soothe me."

Lily smiled at her and Morgan missed a chord or two, shaking her head. "Keep going, keep going," Lily whispered, clapping her hands softly.

"Lily,

Don't you know that you're beautiful?

Your laugh it makes my heart so full

Like a dream, you are magical.

Lily.."

Morgan looked up at her afterward and could feel herself blushing again. "That's all I remember," she admitted, embarrassed. Lily was staring at her intensely, her eyes not wavering. Morgan felt her fingers gently strum over the chords again. As she did, Lily reached over and placed her hands on either side of her face, moving towards her until their lips came together in one fluid motion.

They stayed there for a moment before Morgan pressed back into her. Both of their mouths fell on to one another again and again. When they finally broke away, Morgan stood up to pull Lily from the chair and carry her to the couch. Lily laid in her lap, her arms wrapped around Morgan's neck. As soon as Morgan had sat down, their mouths moved back to one another's in a passionate fury. Lily's hands wrapped into Morgan's curls while Morgan's hands moved up on the curves of her hips.

Morgan kissed her deeply until she moved her mouth across Lily's jaw and onto the side of her neck. She planted her lips into the soft skin there, tasting its dewiness. Lily let out a soft sigh as Morgan's hands trailed up her body.

After a moment, Lily fell down on the couch, Morgan crawling on top of her. Their mouths met again, and Morgan pressed their bodies together, grinding into her. The heat was building inside of her, raging out of control. It had been a long time since she'd been with her this way.

Their mouths met again, and their tongues chased one another till they were gasping for air. Morgan moved her mouth onto her ear, kissing it softly before she made her way down the side of her neck again.

Lily moaned when Morgan's hands worked up the sides of her body. As Morgan slid under the bottom of her shirt and touched the skin of her stomach, Lily erupted into a fit of giggles.

Morgan pulled away, startled, looking down at her. "Are you okay?"

Lily's giggles were so intense that she was nearly crying. Morgan sat up trying to give her room to breathe. "Lily?"

Lily laid there trying to calm herself and catch her breath. Eventually, she was able to, and Morgan helped her sit up on the couch. "I'm sorry," she breathed. Lily pulled her to her mouth again, and they resumed kissing briefly before Morgan pulled away. It was the hardest thing she ever had to do.

"It's weird for you, isn't it?" Morgan asked her. "Being with me?"

Lily looked like she didn't want to answer at first. "You're my best friend," she said awkwardly, putting a hand on Morgan's cheek and stroking it. "I mean, we've known each other since we were kids."

Morgan felt herself fall back on the couch, letting her body try to recover from the intense buildup that had just occurred. Lily stared at her, looking guilty.

"It's okay, Lily," Morgan said, smiling at her. Lily's hand fell on her own and Lily kissed her again. Just for a moment.

"I'm really sorry," she said again. Morgan watched her grimace.

"Are you hurting?" Morgan asked her. Lily hesitated for a moment before she nodded.

"Why didn't you say something sooner?" Morgan asked her, scooping her up from the couch.

"I didn't want to ruin our date," Lily admitted, and Morgan couldn't help but be flattered that she'd put so much thought into it. Still, she worried, leading her carefully back down the hallway into the bedroom. Morgan laid her on the bed before she disappeared back down the hall to fetch her medication and a glass of water.

Lily took it graciously before she spoke again. "What about dinner?"

"I've got an idea," Morgan smiled at her. "Remember, back up plan." She tapped the side of her head a few times. Then she propped Lily up on a pillow, so she was sitting up slightly against the headboard. Once Morgan had gotten her situated, she went back into the kitchen to fetch the food. She plated some and rooted around in the cabinets for a tray. After she'd found one, she brought everything into the bedroom.

"Now," Morgan said as she sat the tray down in front of her. "Lily says we're not supposed to eat in the bedroom. But I won't tell her if you won't."

Lily let out a laugh and smiled as she looked down at the food. "It looks delicious." The two of them worked together to clear the plate, Lily happily eating most of the salmon. When she finished, she looked exhausted. Morgan took the tray back into the kitchen and washed it quickly before returning. When she had, Lily's eyes were closed.

Morgan walked over to her, carefully picking her up to adjust her further down on the bed, so she was laying down. As she did, Lily looked up at her, smiling. "I'm sorry I ruined our date," she said.

"You didn't ruin anything," Morgan smiled back at her, running a hand along the side of her face. She pulled the covers up around her. "Just get some sleep. You'll feel better tomorrow."

"Will you stay here with me?" Lily asked her, wrapping her hand around Morgan's wrist. Without a moment of hesitation, Morgan turned off the lights and fell into bed beside her. Lily took her hand and wrapped it around her, while she pushed their bodies close together. Morgan held onto her tightly, kissing the back of her head as she breathed in her sweet scent.

And into the night, Lily uttered the most beautiful words she could ever speak. "I love you, Morgan." It filled every inch of Morgan to the brim. Even if she hadn't meant it quite the same that Morgan felt for her.

"I love you too," Morgan whispered as she closed her eyes.

The Date

THE FIRST TIME THAT Morgan Wallace went on a date with Lily Taylor, it was out painting. Which greatly confused Lily, because she had no earthly idea how to paint. The two of them took off on the Friday night after they'd gotten back from San Diego to downtown Seattle. They grabbed a bite to eat before they made their way to the bar.

"Why are they holding a painting class at a bar?" Lily wondered aloud as they made their way inside. The group was easy to spot in the back, canvases lined the tables, and some of the couples had already arrived.

"So you can drink," Morgan said as they sat down beside another younger couple. The two of them introduced themselves before they each ordered a beer.

"Inebriation and painting, that sounds fantastic," Lily smiled at her.

"Don't knock it till you try it," Morgan replied, nudging her softly.

As much as Lily joked about the painting class, she did better than she thought she would. Morgan had picked a day when they were learning how to paint seascapes, and Lily turned out to be a natural at it. Just as they were finishing painting the foam on the waves, Lily felt Morgan nudge her on the side. When she turned to face her, Morgan splattered the paintbrush full of blue paint down the side of her face. Some of it landed on her painting

Lily stared at her for a moment while Morgan erupted into a fit of laughter. They'd both had a few beers by then, so even Lily found herself laughing after a moment. They went back to work for a minute or so before Lily turned and painted a stripe of white down Morgan's cheek.

The game went on most of the evening, each of them taking turns splattering each other with paint. By the end of the night, there was more paint on the two of them than there was in their pictures. The instructor did not seem pleased, and they were quick to leave.

The walk back to the train home was spent in a fit of giggles. Lily held on to Morgan's hand as they walked. They toted their finished paintings in the other. When they reached the train station, it was mostly barren. They found a bench and waited, still laughing about the night's events.

Lily turned to look at Morgan, who she found staring at her rather intensely. "What?" She asked, brushing a strand of stray hair behind her ear.

"You look like a Picasso painting," Morgan said, stifling a laugh.

"You mean Pollock," Lily corrected her with a smile.

The two of them sat on the bench together for a while in silence. Lily felt Morgan run her hand gently over hers, stroking it with her fingertips. It sent a little shiver down her spine.

"Hey, Lily," Morgan finally said, leaning in to whisper in her ear.

"Mm?" She replied, her breath quickening as she felt Morgan's lips barely graze her skin.

"You're my Picasso," Morgan whispered, and Lily could feel her smiling.

"You're my Pollock," Lily corrected her again and turned to look towards her. The two stared deeply at one another, their mouths so close together that Lily could feel the tickle of Morgan's lips against hers. They lingered there for a moment before Lily felt Morgan's lips fall onto her own. The kiss was so subtle it was as if it hardly had happened. But it had stirred her.

Morgan smirked when she pulled away for a moment, and Lily found herself wrapping her hand around the collar of Morgan's shirt and pulling her back towards her again, planting their lips together. They moved together in unison, their mouths crashing together over and over before Lily grew brave enough to taste her. Their tongues chased one another. Lily felt Morgan's hands at her waist, and it sent a shiver up her.

After they both were breathless, Morgan leaned into the side of her neck, putting her mouth to her ear.

"I want you," Morgan Wallace begged her softly. And at that moment, Lily Taylor realized, she wanted her too.

Chapter Six
Lily

EARLY TUESDAY MORNING, the day after Lily visited Morgan to help with the lighthouse repairs, she was awoken by her brother. He shook her shoulder softly.

"Hey Lil," John whispered, and when Lily opened her eyes, she could see the sun barely starting to peek over the horizon. "Would you want to go with me to the bookstore today?"

It took Lily a moment to realize what he had asked. Eventually, she yawned and nodded, sitting up in bed. As she did every morning, she wiggled her toes for a moment and then did her best to try and move her legs. Today she felt them shift the slightest bit and it sent a wave of happiness through her. It only happened once, but it was enough to put her in a great mood.

Elise made them both pancakes that morning, and Lily ate more than she'd likely ever ate in her life. So much so that her brother teased her for it and told her to "leave some for the pregnant lady and her babies."

After they'd helped clean up and Elise had fixed John a tea and Lily a coffee to go, they loaded up in the car and took off down the tree-lined street towards downtown. While they drove, John listened to the news and argued with nearly every story about one thing or another.

"You know, you should really consider listening to classical music when you drive," Lily said, laughing. "It would help your blood pressure." John rolled his eyes at her as he turned into the parking lot of the store. The sign across the front read *Books by the Ocean*. It looked as magical and as perfect as it had the last time Lily remembered seeing it. The building looked like it had been freshly painted too. An off-white that made the blue lettering of the store sign pop.

John rolled her up onto the sidewalk before he let the wheelchair go and Lily proceeded to move up to the store. He unlocked the doors and held them open for her. When Lily went inside, she basked in the quaint feel of it. "You moved things around," she noticed as she rolled down the aisles.

"Last year," John said, nodding. "It was time for a change. You and Morgan helped a lot." Lily wasn't the least bit surprised. John wasn't the type to sit still for long. He'd always enjoyed a little variety, and it hadn't been the first time he'd switched the place up.

"I like it," Lily complimented him as she ran her fingers over the large selection of used books in the back of the store. "Although I really think you should consider putting all these amazing books up front."

"Gotta make some money, Lil." John said clapping his hands together. "I'm going to open. Do you mind helping me stock some new stuff that came in today? It'll keep you busy."

Lily thought of what Morgan had said that day she'd come over to help with the lighthouse. *I think you're the first person in the world who's ever been so excited to do house repairs.* She couldn't help but feel the same way about working with her brother. The thought of being useful thrilled her.

When John said she'd be busy, it had been an understatement. He'd gotten such a large shipment of books, it took Lily nearly the entire morning to shelve them all. When she had finished, she spent time organizing the display shelves and cleaning up the store. They took a quick break to eat lunch, and Lily took her medication when she started to feel a little pain coming on. John fussed over her continuing to work, but he gave in when she argued with him.

In the early afternoon, as Lily was organizing used books in the back of the store, she caught a glance at a familiar face she hadn't seen in years. Jacob Elkins was a historian and professor that had worked with John and Lily's father at the university. If there had ever been another soul on the planet that loved books as much as her brother and her father, it was Jacob.

"Jacob, is that you?" Lily heard her brother call out to him as he wandered inside. The two embraced for a moment, smiling at one another.

"I heard a rumor that you'd opened a bookstore a few years ago," Jacob said, casting his eyes across the room. "I can't believe I hadn't heard of it till recently."

"Better late than never, right?"

As they chatted, Lily came up beside her brother. Jacob finally looked down, and for a moment she had trouble reading his expression. Finally, he spoke. "Lily?"

"Hi, Jacob," Lily smiled, offering him a handshake. "It's good to see you."

"You look more and more like your mother every day," he admitted, and Lily felt a wave of emotions crash into her with the thought of it. She smiled as he leaned down to offer her a hug. By the look on his face, she could tell he was wondering what had happened to her.

"Boating accident," Lily explained. The air was awkward for a moment before John offered to show him around the building.

As they made their way through the shelves of books, her brother and Jacob got lost in conversation. When they rounded a corner, Jacob stopped in his tracks, staring at a glass case on the wall. Inside was a book that Lily did not recognize.

"Is that an EE Cummings anthology?" He asked, looking at John. "A *signed* EE Cummings anthology?"

John smiled, looking down at Lily. "It is. Lily found it at an estate sale a year ago."

Lily stared at her brother in shock. "I did?" When John nodded, she couldn't believe it. Her brother took it from the case, handing it to Jacob to look at. Lily looked and saw that it, in fact, was a signed copy of the book. "Who would sell a signed copy?"

"Someone who didn't know what they were selling, apparently."

"I met EE Cummings once," Jacob said, looking at John and then Lily. "At a book conference in Maryland. Very nice fellow. I always regretted not getting his autograph for my collection. This is certainly a treasure."

John smiled, taking the book when it was handed back to him. Lily stared at it in disbelief as he set it back in the case.

"So what do you do now?" Her brother asked Jacob as they went back towards the front of the store. "Do you still work for the historical society?"

"Would you believe I'm the president? They elected me last year."

Jacob stayed a good while, chatting mostly with John while Lily finished working in the back of the store. When he finally took his leave, he came back to say goodbye to Lily.

"Come visit sometime," Jacob said, smiling down at her. "I'd love to see you and your brother again soon."

THE NEXT DAY, LILY went back to physical therapy and was escorted by John and Morgan, both who were as anxious as she was. Again that morning, she felt the tiniest bit of movements in her legs. They moved upward, just the smallest touch, but this time she was sure it was real. The whole drive to Portland, Lily moved them as much as she possibly could.

Carmela was in an extra good mood that day. This had been the third therapy session with her. After Lily had explained about the subtle movement in her feet, Carmela looked even happier, if that were possible.

"We're going to try something new today," Carmela said as Tom helped her out of the wheelchair. He brought her to a harness that was suspended from the ceiling, and he and Carmela worked together to strap her into it. It was the first time since the accident that she stood almost completely vertical. It sent an intense pain through her entire body but she was so excited about the idea of actually standing, she ignored it. Instead, she felt tears rolling down her cheeks.

She stood in between two railings, and Carmela helped her grasp hold of both of them. Morgan and John were beaming at her.

"How does it feel to be standing?" Carmela smiled at her.

"I can't believe it," Lily gasped, still crying.

"Well, I'll let you take it in for a minute, but we're not done yet." Carmela moved, so she was facing in front of Lily, between the bars. "Let's see if we can get your leg to move even just a little bit for us. What do you say?" Lily nodded, her hands grasped around the railing tightly. The harness took nearly all the weight off of her feet, so she felt as if she was almost floating.

"You ready?" Carmela asked her after they all spent a moment in silence. Lily nodded, unsure if she really was but wanting to try anyway. "Alright, let's try to move that leg."

Lily concentrated as hard as she could, closing her eyes and feeling her leg beneath her. For a while, nothing happened, and Lily began getting discouraged. Then suddenly she heard Morgan gasp when her whole entire foot gave a little twitch and her leg kicked outward just the tiniest amount. Once she'd moved one, she attempted the other and found it easier this time.

"Holy shit," Morgan said and then quickly covered her mouth.

Lily let out another cry, mostly from happiness, but also because the pain was starting to become unbearable. Carmela took the hint and both she and Tom removed her from the harness and sat her back into the wheelchair. A wave of emotions rushed through Lily after they'd set her down. She cried again, wiping the tears from her eyes.

"How did that feel?" Carmela asked her, squeezing her shoulder.

Morgan rushed to Lily and squatted down in front of her. "Lily, that was amazing." Lily looked up at her, and the two embraced for a moment. As she was pulling away, Lily's hands wrapped around the sides of Morgan's face, and for a moment time stood still. It seems as if they both wanted the same thing, moving their faces together. Just as they drew close, Lily felt the fear of judgment wash over her and quickly pulled away, clearing her throat. She caught the hint of disappointment on Morgan's face, but it was replaced with the genuine happiness of her accomplishment. "I'm so proud of you," she said as John came over to pat her on the back.

The successful therapy visit had Lily on a high the rest of the day. They enjoyed lunch together again at the pier. John grew so annoyed with Lily stealing his fries that he ordered her an entire basket for herself, which she devoured happily. They went for a drive around Portland afterward, and by the time they were headed back, the adrenaline had started to wear off, and Lily found herself falling asleep.

WHEN LILY WOKE THE day after her failed date with Morgan, she found herself wrapped tightly in her arms, still at the lighthouse. Morgan's soft breathing echoed in her ear while she slept. It was late. Lily wondered if she had even gotten up to do the chores around the house, but she was too content to wake her and ask. Instead, she laid there, staring out the windows. She listened to the sounds of the ocean crashing along the rocky shoreline and the caws of seagulls flying overhead. She didn't think she could feel more relaxed.

Lily snuggled closer to Morgan, feeling their bodies push together when she did. Morgan pushed back, squeezing her tightly with her arm. A moment later, Lily felt the gentle graze of lips tickling her earlobe and the side of her face.

"Good morning," Morgan whispered to her, covering the side of her face with small soft kisses. Lily sighed, rolling over so that Morgan's face loomed above hers. They stared at each other for a long time, Lily enjoying those beautiful big green eyes watching her so lovingly. Neither of them spoke for a moment. Finally, Lily reached her hand up to the side of Morgan's face, pulling her down to meet her. They kissed briefly.

"Did you get up this morning?" Lily asked her when they parted.

Morgan shook her head, smiling. "There was no way in the world I was leaving *this*." The way she said it made Lily blush slightly and they kissed again.

"We better get to work then," Lily said, placing her hand on Morgan's cheek.

Much to Morgan's displeasure, the two of them rose from the bed and worked together to get the chores done in the morning. This time,

Morgan let Lily help clean the reflective panels and raise the flag all on her own. Close to lunchtime, there was a knock at the front door.

"I really hope that isn't John," Lily said, and Morgan smirked at her when she said it.

"It's not. I have a surprise for you." Morgan wandered down the steps and answered the door. A few minutes later, two men hauled in several boxes. When they left, Morgan sat on the floor inspecting them.

"What is that?" Lily asked curiously from the kitchen table. Morgan fetched a knife to open one, and when she did, there were beautiful black cabinet doors inside that matched the black countertops in the kitchen. Lily looked at her, still confused.

"So," Morgan explained as she got back to her feet. "You have been begging me for months to fix the cabinets. If you hadn't noticed, they're in dire need of a makeover." Lily looked up at the cabinets around the kitchen. They were a bit dated, and some were a little crooked.

"You've had your eye on these for a while, and I promised you we'd get to them soon, but it kept getting pushed back due to other things. I thought I'd fix them for you now."

Lily stared at her in disbelief before she smiled at her, shaking her head.

"What?" Morgan asked as she started to unwrap the cabinet doors from their packaging and line them up in the kitchen.

"You're just wonderful," Lily said simply. "Can you get me my wheelchair? I want to help."

The two spent the next few hours switching out the cabinet doors. Lily would hold onto the doors and various tools while Morgan worked. Once again, Lily's tastes in decorating were impeccable. The new doors looked fantastic. The two were nearly finished when there was another knock at the door.

"Now *that* might be your brother," Morgan said as she sat down the door she was about to hang. Lily watched her as she disappeared down the steps again. When she heard the voices of an older man and woman, she wondered for a moment if it was Abigail and Richard. Finally, she heard the tinge of a British accent and knew they must have been visitors.

"Let me go open the door, and I'll bring you guys right on up." Morgan shut the door for a moment and walked back up the stairs to Lily. "You want to come see me in action?"

"Someone's here for a tour?" Lily asked curiously, and Morgan nodded. When Lily smiled, Morgan scooped her up from the seat and took her up to the top of the lighthouse. Once she'd settled her on the side of the windowsill, Morgan looked back at her.

"I'll be right back," she said, kissing her softly on the lips before she disappeared back down the steps. A few minutes later, the three of them had made it to the top.

"This is Lily," Morgan introduced her. Lily didn't think she had ever seen such an adorable looking couple. They looked to be in their late fifties or early sixties. They both were holding hands when they reached the top of the steps, but neither of them was out of breath, both in great shape for their age.

"Pleasure to meet you," Lily said, shaking their hands.

"Oh, what a view," the man's hint of accent came out while he admired the scenery. Finally, he turned back to Morgan. "How old is she?"

"The Wallace Lighthouse was built in 1891," Morgan said with a smile. "It's been in the same family for generations now. While it's not officially used like it was years ago, it still operates as a traditional lighthouse. The beacon shines every night, and we keep track of the boats in the harbor."

The couple looked fascinated. Lily watched Morgan as she explained about the work she did each day, and about the history of lighthouses. It was intoxicating to see the way her eyes lit up when she talked about it. The way she smiled. Everything about her seemed alive and energized. It was as if Lily was seeing her for the very first time again in Ms. Penny's third-grade class, talking about how she wanted to work in the lighthouse when she was older.

After Morgan had taken the guests back downstairs, Lily looked out the windows at the rocky beaches below. It was a beautiful day outside, not a cloud in sight. A seagull perched on the railing out on the top of the lighthouse, staring at her. She still couldn't imagine how she'd ever hate it here.

Morgan came back a few minutes later and apologized for taking so long. Lily smiled at her, and when Morgan leaned down to pick her up, Lily put her hands on either side of her face and kissed her deeply. Morgan sighed happily, pressing back against her and pushing Lily into the glass window behind her. When they finally broke apart, they both were smiling.

LILY SPENT SUNDAY WITH John and Elise, who both had requested her help in doing final preparations for the babies. Elise was due at any moment and spent most of the time instructing John and Lily on what needed to be done. They picked up some last minute items from the store, cleaned the nursery and other rooms, and John double checked the hospital bag to make sure it was ready to go.

When Monday came, Morgan picked her up bright and early, toting a beautiful black business dress over her arm. The two worked together to get Lily dressed, and Morgan waited for her as she fixed her hair and makeup. When Lily came out from the downstairs bathroom, Morgan stared at her, smiling.

"You look fantastic," she said, and Lily felt herself blush.

The drive to Portland was mostly quiet. Morgan did her best to distract her with casual conversation every once in a while, but Lily was still nervous regardless. As they drove onto streets Lily didn't recognize, she suddenly saw the sign that signaled their entrance to the research park. It was on the outskirts of town, and the building Lily worked in was right on the edge of the water. It was a beautiful place, filled with large glass windows on every side. There was a dock adjacent to the building housing several boats.

Morgan parked the car and let Lily situate herself into the wheelchair. The building was very modern and had large sliding glass doors that were perfect for Lily to navigate through. When they got inside, a woman behind the front desk beamed at her.

"Oh my gosh, you're here!" She jumped to her feet excitedly, her high pitch voice echoing around the room. It was a swanky looking place, with an exorbitant looking waiting area that was entirely too white. The walls were painted with beautiful murals of the ocean. A video was playing on a large flat-screen TV on the far side of the room, showing a group of researchers out on the water. As Lily watched it for a moment, she realized she was one of the researchers in the video.

"This is Becky," Morgan introduced her as the perky blond woman came to meet her, she squatted down beside the wheelchair, placing a hand on top of Lily's.

"I'm so glad you're here. We missed you." Becky hugged her tightly. Lily patted her back gently. "Let me call Bill and Ryan. They'll be so excited to see you." Becky got to her feet and walked around to the other side of the desk. When she'd put her phone to her ear, Morgan leaned down next to Lily and whispered softly to her.

"Becky's the receptionist. You like her. She brings you sweets all the time, and then you come home and complain how you've eaten too much sugar."

Lily laughed a little before Becky hung up the phone and smiled at them. "They're finishing up a meeting. Would you like to see your office?" Lily nodded, and the three of them took off down the hallway. Lily didn't have to ask which one was hers. As soon as she saw the "Get Well" banner and the balloons and flowers that were strewn about, she knew.

"Do you need anything? Are you thirsty? I can get you some water." Becky looked down at Lily who did her best to smile back at her.

"I'm fine. Thanks though."

Becky nodded, smiling back. "I'm so glad you're here. We really missed you." Lily wished she could say the same. Instead, she offered thanks before Becky left Morgan and her alone in the office. Lily admired the get well cards and flowers that lined her desk. As she read through them, Morgan told her about her coworkers and what she knew of them.

When Lily was about through reading, there was a knock at the door. Two men stood out in the hallway. One had a beefy build and sported a brown-haired goatee. He had the friendliest smile Lily had ever seen.

The other man was tall and lanky, with sandy blonde hair. He wore a t-shirt that described the different kinds of sharks.

"You're here!" The lanky man said, squatting down to meet her. Lily smiled at him as best she could and stuck out her hand.

"I'm Lily," she said and then realized how awkward she must have sounded. Of course, he knew who she was. He stared at her for a moment trying to process the situation before he smiled at her.

"I'm Bill," the man said, shaking her hand. "I'm the research team manager." Lily studied him over for a minute before he continued to speak. "And this is Ryan," he looked up at the stockier man standing above him. "He's the assistant research team manager."

Lily smiled at them. "Nice to meet you."

Bill offered to take Lily on a tour of the place. The views through the windows were spectacular. Most of them looked out at the ocean or the rocky beaches. It reminded Lily a lot of the views from the lighthouse. In the basement there was a huge wall of glass that looked out under the Atlantic, offering a view of the ocean floor and some of the marine life.

"Is that Atlantic salmon?" Lily asked, noticing a collection of fish that swam by the glass. "I was working on a thesis paper in school about them." She found herself trailing off when she thought about school.

When she met Ryan's gaze, he was smiling at her. "That's actually our current research project. We've been working on tracking their feeding frequency. You've been a huge help." Lily was fascinated, turning her attention back out into the ocean for a moment.

As they made their way back up to the main floor, Lily found herself overwhelmed with her co-workers approaching her. It felt like she didn't get a minutes rest as they walked, someone always offering her a hug or asking her how she was feeling. They all seemed to know her well, whereas Lily tried desperately to remember anything about them and couldn't. By the time they reached her office, Lily had sworn if another person asked her if she remembered them, she might snap.

Once they'd all made it inside, Bill closed the door behind them and he and Ryan took a seat. Morgan leaned against her desk, crossing her arms.

"So, what do you think?" Bill asked.

Lily pondered for a moment before she responded. "It's really nice." She didn't quite know what else to say.

"I'm sure it's probably a little overwhelming," Bill said, smiling at her. A little overwhelming was an understatement, but Lily did her best to maintain her composure. "We just wanted to let you know that we'll support you in whatever you decide. And we'll accommodate you however you need."

Lily looked at Morgan for a moment and then back to Ryan and Bill. She took a deep breath before she spoke. "I don't really remember much of my marine biology classes," she admitted painfully. "All I know is one semester. I don't know how much use I'll be."

Bill nodded and reached out to put a hand over hers. "Lily, we'll do whatever we need to do to help you succeed. You don't have to worry about that. We have plenty of work that you can handle if you wanted to come back."

"Bill and I even have some contacts at the University of Maine who offered to let you take some classes remotely to get you up to speed." Ryan and Lily exchanged a glance. "And you have plenty of folks willing to help you here if you need it. We're all here for you."

Lily didn't know what to say. There were so many thoughts racing through her head that she was having trouble focusing. When she looked up at Morgan, it was clear that she realized Lily was feeling overwhelmed.

"She'll think about it," Morgan said to them, offering a smile. Both of the men nodded.

"Let us know what we can do to help you," Bill said, patting her hand again before he moved back to get to his feet. Ryan followed suit. Lily smiled at them as best she could, and they said their goodbyes before they left Lily and Morgan alone.

As soon as they had, Lily felt herself start to hyperventilate. She buried her face in her hands as tears started to stream from her eyes.

"Lily," Morgan sounded panicked, squatting down beside her. "What is going on?" Lily found that she couldn't answer, only struggle to breathe.

"Hey, hey, hey," Morgan said, somewhat sternly. "Okay. You need to breathe. Put your head between your legs. Come on, Lily." Lily felt her push down on her back and Lily folded over. As soon as she did, she could already start to feel her body relax. It took a minute or two, but eventually, her breaths became ragged but somewhat back to normal. "There we go," Morgan said, relieved. "Can you talk to me now?"

Lily looked up at her, feeling rather miserable. "I don't think I can do this."

"That's okay," Morgan said, running her hand down Lily's back. "This is completely your decision. Nobody is asking you to do anything."

"Morgan, I didn't know any of them. I don't know where I am." Lily felt herself starting to cry again. "I don't remember anything."

Morgan hesitated for a moment before she responded. "I know."

Lily sighed, wiping her face with the back of her hand. "Can we go?" Morgan stood up and gathered most of Lily's cards and some of the flowers from the desk. She used her free hand to open up the door.

Becky stared at her as she passed by the reception desk. She gave a small wave. "Hope you feel better soon. It was really good to see you." It was the polite thing to say, but it made Lily ache all the more.

The whole drive back to Kennebunkport, Lily cried off and on. Morgan took her hand as they drove back, squeezing it softly. When they reached the house, John met them in the driveway. When he saw Lily's disheveled state, he looked concerned.

"Not the best experience," Morgan admitted as John scooped his sister from the car. Lily leaned against his chest, sniffling loudly. She watched as Morgan came around the car, swept her hair from Lily's face, and then gently kissed her on the forehead. "I'll call later?"

Lily nodded. "I'm sorry, Morgan."

"Don't be," she said, resting her hand on Lily's cheek for a moment.

John gave her a nod before he walked into the house. Lily requested to be taken to her room, and her brother obliged, laying her down on the bed. After he covered her with the bedsheets, he sat down on the side of the bed, stroking the top of her head. "Do you need anything?"

Lily shook her head. "I'm fine. I want to be left alone."

John understood, kissing her softly on the forehead before he stood up to take his leave. After he shut the door, Lily found herself crying yet again. She forced herself to roll over so she could stare out the window. Her mind drifted for a while until finally, she fell asleep.

It was nearing eleven in the morning the next day when John came back. He shook her until she turned to look up at him. "It's time to get up, Lil," he said sternly. Lily pulled the sheets over her head and rolled away from him. As soon as she did, her brother tugged roughly until they flew off of her again. Lily groaned loudly. "I didn't come home from work for nothing. You aren't going to pout all day. Now let's get up. Elise is going to help you get dressed and then we're going to eat some lunch."

Lily, who looked slightly humiliated, let Elise help her into a t-shirt and sweatpants and then the two of them made their way into the kitchen. John was finishing plating some grilled cheese sandwiches and tomato soup. When he sat it in front of her, Lily looked down at it for a moment, unsure if she even had an appetite.

"Eat," her brother said when he sat down beside her.

"Sweetheart, let her be," Elise said, putting a hand on his arm.

Lily sighed, taking a bite of the sandwich after she'd dipped it in the soup. Surprisingly, she found that she was hungrier than she thought. She'd nearly been in bed a whole day, so her stomach was appreciative of the food.

"Morgan has been calling me non-stop this morning. You need to call her back." John and Lily met eyes. She nodded at him before she took another bite of food. While Lily ate in silence, John and Elise chatted until they'd all finished their meals. Afterward, Lily helped load the dishes into the dishwasher while her brother wiped down the kitchen table. By that time, she'd started to feel a little better.

Just as he was about to leave, John kissed Elise goodbye and then his sister on the top of her head. "Don't go back to sleep," he said sternly, and Lily nodded. "And call Morgan." As he turned to head out the door, Lily called out to him.

"Hey John," she said, and he turned back to look at her. "Thanks." Her brother smiled at her briefly before he took his leave.

Lily helped Elise with chores around the house to keep herself busy that afternoon. When her phone rang close to dinner time, she finally realized she'd forgotten to call Morgan.

"Hello?" Lily answered, putting the phone to her ear.

"Are you okay?" Morgan asked her. "I've been trying to get a hold of you all day."

Lily felt guilty for not having called her back sooner. "I'm sorry, Morgan. I'm not having a very good day."

Morgan paused for a moment before she spoke again. "I kind of figured. Mind if I try to make it a little bit better? I have a surprise for you." Lily couldn't help but smile a little when she said it. It seemed that Morgan was full of surprises lately. Sometimes she didn't know what she ever did to deserve it.

"Okay," Lily said.

"Come out when you're ready, I'm waiting outside."

Lily was about to offer a surprised response when she heard the phone hang up on the other end. She called Elise and let her know she was leaving before she headed out the door.

Morgan was waiting outside, leaning against her car. When they met eyes, she smiled broadly, giving a wave.

"What are you doing here?" Lily called out to her as she made her way down the sidewalk. When she reached the car, Morgan opened the passenger side door for her and Lily moved into the car carefully.

"Like I said, I have a surprise for you." As soon as she shut the door, Morgan toted Lily's wheelchair to the back of the car and then hopped inside. They made their way back to the lighthouse, making mostly small talk. Lily apologized at least a half-dozen times on the way, though Morgan constantly told her it was fine.

When they reached the driveway and Morgan had gotten out to open the passenger side door for Lily, she looked down at her for a moment. "Okay, you have to close your eyes now." They looked at each other for a moment, Lily studying her face curiously. Finally, she did as she was told and she felt Morgan wrap her arms around her and hold her close. She made her way up the stairway, and Lily felt as she put her down on the couch. "Keep them closed, I'll be right back."

Lily heard Morgan disappear down the steps again outside and a few moments later return, dragging up the wheelchair by the sound of it. She sat Lily in it once more before she cleared her throat. "Okay, you can open them."

Everything suddenly came into view around her, and it took Lily a minute to realize what she was seeing. The room was filled with neon paper. Sticky notes. Attached to nearly everything. Lily rolled herself around in a circle, unsure of what to think.

"Go look," Morgan said, nodding towards a wall that was covered. She approached a picture of a starfish. When she reached it, she pulled the note hanging on it off and read it quietly.

Our senior year you wished upon this very starfish. I told you that your wish would come true, and it did. We moved here.

Lily looked at Morgan curiously and moved down the wall to another. This time it was stuck on the window. *Winter. Our first snowstorm here. It snowed so much that it came up to this window. We were stuck inside all weekend. We made hot chocolate and watched cheesy Hallmark movies.*

Morgan handed her the one that was attached to the floor in front of her when she saw it. *Where we spent our first night. We didn't sleep much, but it was my favorite night with you.*

Lily moved around the house, pulling note after note off of everything imaginable. A house that was full of memories.

Where we put our first Christmas tree. You decorated it of course.

I spilled coffee on your beautiful rug and spent all afternoon trying to clean it. When you got home, you laughed and told me you wanted a new one anyway.

A grandfather clock hung on the wall. It was old and weathered, but Lily recognized it when she saw it. "I've seen this before," she said, reaching up to run her hand across it. "It was here when we used to come as kids. Except it was on that wall over there." Lily pointed over towards the stairs and the front door. *My grandfather's favorite clock. He used to tell you it was a "grandfather clock" and you'd reply. "That's right! It's your clock!"* Lily laughed again.

Another hung on the paintings in the bedroom. The one from their first date. *You're my Picasso.* It read. Lily looked back at Morgan, and she smiled at her and shrugged.

It took over an hour for Lily to get through all the notes spread across the house. Morgan took her up into the lighthouse to find more, and even out onto the docks. Sometimes when she'd come to one, Morgan would explain the context behind it. Other times, it remained a mystery. When they'd come back inside, Lily looked at her in disbelief.

"I can't believe you did all of this," she said, breathlessly. Every one of the notes was clutched in her hand tightly.

Morgan sat down in front of her, taking Lily's hands into her own. "I know you think that you're missing out on all these things. All these moments that we had. All these moments from your life before your accident. I can't begin to know what that is like." Morgan paused for a moment, looking at her. "But Lily, look at all the memories we had in a year here." She squeezed her hands, holding the notes. "That was just one year. One year of so much more we'll have together. God, I was so scared that night I found you on the beach that I'd never get any more to share with you. And here you are. And I promise I'll spend the rest of our days filling that head of yours with all the memories you could ever want."

Morgan leaned into her, resting their heads together. Lily breathed her in, feeling tears streaming down her face. They sat there for a while before they both looked up at one another. Lily wrapped her hands around the side of Morgan's face and ran her thumbs across her cheeks.

"I love you, Morgan Wallace," she said, and it was the truest words she'd ever spoken.

"I love you too, Lily Taylor," Morgan replied, smiling as she wiped the tears from Lily's eyes.

Just as she did, Lily pulled them together, so their mouths collided softly. Lily had never felt so much emotion pouring from her in her life. She held Morgan close as their lips met over and over again, growing stronger and more deliberate with each kiss.

"Take me to our bedroom," Lily whispered to her when their mouths broke. Morgan lifted her carefully from the wheelchair and held her close as they made their way down the hall. When Lily was laid down on the sheets, she looked up to Morgan, who stared down at her with her big green eyes as she pulled herself on top of her. Their mouths moved together again, tenderly. So soft and subtle that it tickled Lily's lips when they kissed. After a while, Morgan tasted her, and their tongues moved between their mouths, teasing each other.

When they broke for a moment, Morgan looked down at Lily as she stroked her cheek with her fingers. The way she looked at her made Lily shiver. Morgan's mouth drew onto her cheek, planting kisses down to her earlobe and then onto her neckline. Lily wrapped her arms around her, pulling her close as Morgan worked into her skin. Every touch shot waves of electricity through her. Morgan's hands moved up Lily's body, running along her hips and curves. Finally, they fell back down at the edges of Lily's shirt and paused there. They shared a look before Lily propped herself up and Morgan slid her hands underneath the fabric, rolling it off of her body in one fell swoop.

When Lily fell back against the bed, her body was filled with goose-bumps. She shivered slightly, watching as Morgan's eyes trailed over her exposed skin, taking in every detail. Morgan sat up carefully on her legs, being sure not to put too much of her weight on Lily. Morgan's hands gently ran down her skin, from her shoulders, down the lengths of her arms, from her collarbone, over her breasts and down to her stomach. Lily closed her eyes and fell into every stroke she made.

Morgan moved her mouth back over the top of Lily's for a moment, sharing a deep and passionate kiss. When they broke, they looked at each other and Morgan stroked her cheek. "You're so beautiful," she said softly. Lily wrapped her hand into Morgan's curls as she felt her move her mouth down onto her neck and into her collarbone. Lily lifted herself up once more so Morgan could unclasp her bra. Another shiver rolled through her as Morgan moved her lips into the flesh of her breasts, covering them in kisses. She pulled one into her mouth, and Lily gasped, her fingers clutching around Morgan's head as she worked. Once she'd pleasured them both, Morgan continued her kisses over the flesh of Lily's stomach, drawing her fingers along as her mouth moved over her. Each touch she gave sent Lily into more and more of a frenzy.

Finally, Morgan reached Lily's pants, and she paused, looking up at her. Lily felt a pit growing in the center of her stomach and stared down at her.

"Morgan," Lily put a hand on her shoulder and the two met eyes. "What if I can't?" She felt embarrassed even asking.

Morgan crawled up to lay softly on top of her again, staring down at her with her captivating green eyes. She leaned down, putting her lips to Lily's ear. "Lily," she whispered, and then she described in vivid detail the things she intended to do. Every touch she'd make. It made Lily ache inside. "Just relax," Morgan said, kissing her neck. "And trust me."

When they looked into each other's eyes again, Morgan ran her fingers down the side of Lily's cheek and drew her lips down the length of her body. Lily shivered, her breaths growing more and more ragged with each touch. Morgan stroked her breasts again until her nipples were hard. She flicked them with her tongue until Lily moaned with pleasure. Then Morgan's mouth moved down her stomach and her hands wrapped around the elastic band of Lily's pants.

The two worked together to relieve her of the rest of her clothing. Lily could barely feel the touch of Morgan's fingers as they trailed down the length of her legs. When they came up towards her middle, Lily's breath began to quicken. Morgan paused for a moment, crawling on top of her again to fetch a pillow. She propped Lily up on it. After, Morgan drew her hands under her shirt, pulling it from her body. Lily watched as she unclasped her bra and then leaned into her. Their breasts rubbed together as Morgan pushed into her body and let her mouth come into the crook of Lily's neck once more. She licked her velvety skin and rubbed their naked flesh together until Lily could feel her nipples hardening between them.

They met lips again, and their tongues lapped at each other hungrily. Morgan reached for Lily's hand and slid it slowly into her pants, letting her feel the wetness between her legs. Once again it made Lily quiver. She let her fingers stroke Morgan, and she moaned softly into Lily's ear. Every part of Lily burned like an untamed fire. Her hand moved faster. More assertively. Their mouths met, and they kissed so deeply neither of them could breathe. It only took moments before Morgan was gasping, her body convulsing.

Morgan moaned into the room. Lily could feel her twitching as her fingers slowed. Morgan ground herself into Lily's fingers as the pleasure rolled through her. Everything she did made Lily ache for her own release.

Morgan planted her mouth against Lily's ear, flicking her earlobe with her tongue. Lily could still hear her ragged breaths as she tried to recover. Morgan's hand stroked down Lily's body while her lips moved over her skin. When she reached the tuff of hair before Lily's middle, she looked up at her. Lily looked at her almost pleadingly, feeling her insides raging out of control. Morgan carefully spread her legs apart. Then they met eyes again. Lily could feel her breath against her. At first, when Morgan's mouth moved into her, she thought she'd feel nothing. Then a sudden movement of Morgan's tongue lit every piece of her up.

"There," Lily gasped loudly, reaching down to push Morgan into her. Morgan worked against her with her mouth, while her fingers raked softly down the flesh of Lily's stomach. The feeling made Lily crazy. "Keep going," Lily begged her, the crest of the wave about to hit her. She closed her eyes, focusing on the rhythmic laps of Morgan's tongue against her until her body began to quiver. When Lily released, her entire body shook. She could even feel it running through her legs.

Even the small amount of pain she'd been feeling disappeared when the waves of ecstasy overcame her. She moaned into the room, her hands gripped tightly into Morgan's curls. Morgan didn't stop until she'd completely relaxed into the bed, panting softly.

As Lily laid catching her breath, Morgan came up beside her and pulled her into her arms. The two kissed for a moment. After Lily's heart had calmed down, she met eyes with Morgan, and the two of them smiled at one another.

"You are filthy, Morgan Wallace," Lily laughed, nudging their noses together.

"I read up on some things. About helping you with your injuries." Morgan admitted with a shrug. "I wanted to make sure it felt good for you. They said using your imagination really helps." While Lily could have interpreted her research as a bad thing, instead she felt rather flattered that Morgan had gone through the trouble.

"Really?" Lily asked her, curiously. "What else did it say?"

Morgan gave her a playful smile and kissed her. "We'd have to go again if you wanted to know."

Lily smirked, running her fingers down the side of Morgan's cheek. She could still feel the lingering sensation of the pleasure she'd just had coursing through her. Morgan leaned over and kissed her on the side of her face and into her neck. "Although I wouldn't be opposed to that if that's what you wanted." Lily let out a soft sigh in response, feeling the heat rise in her all over again.

As Morgan and Lily's mouths moved together again in a passionate fury, a phone rang down the hall. When they pulled apart, Morgan gasped. "Don't worry about it." They moved together again, their hands sweeping over each other's nakedness. Lily cupped Morgan's breasts in her hands and rolled her nipples with her fingertips. Morgan pushed against her, her tongue so far down Lily's throat that neither of them had room to breathe. Just as she climbed on top of Lily, the phone rang again.

"I swear to God if that's your brother—" Morgan gasped for air when they parted. Lily laughed and placed a hand on the side of Morgan's face. "I guess I better go grab it. Hold on." Morgan leaned down and kissed her deeply for a moment before she scampered off the bed and down the hall. When she returned, she was shaking her head.

"Your brother has called four times," Morgan grumbled, handing Lily the phone. A worried look spread across Lily's face as she quickly dialed him back.

"Lily," John answered the phone almost immediately. He sounded panicked. "You need to come to the hospital."

"John, what's going on?" Lily asked him, pushing herself to an upright position on the bed. Morgan sat beside her, looking concerned.

"It's Elise," John said, taking deep breaths into the phone. "She's in labor."

The Starfish

FROM THE MOMENT MORGAN Wallace told Lily Taylor to wish upon a picture of a starfish, hanging in a department store window, she knew it would come true. The two of them had been walking in downtown Seattle after a date. It was two weeks before their college graduation, and they were constantly daydreaming about where their lives would take them next.

"Let's make a move to Hawaii together and be marine biologists," Lily said, kissing Morgan's cheek as they walked. "Like we've dreamed since we started school."

Morgan laughed. "Do you know how expensive it is to live in Hawaii?"

A smirk spread across her face when Lily responded. "I bet I could convince you to move to Hawaii with me."

"Oh really?" Morgan grinned as Lily pushed her into the wall of a brick building, planting their lips together fiercely. A couple walked by watching them, but Lily didn't mind. When they parted, Morgan sighed. "Okay, I'll go wherever you want to go."

As they began walking again, past the glass windows of a department store, Morgan and Lily spotted a beautiful photo of a starfish hanging on display. Morgan paused, tugging at Lily gently. "Make a wish. Anywhere you want to go."

Lily's eyes went from the photo back to Morgan. "A starfish? Are you serious?"

"It's like a star," Morgan shrugged, smiling at her. "Just do it. Close your eyes."

Lily closed her eyes and pondered for a moment before she thought of what she wanted. When she'd finished, she looked to Morgan and smiled. "That was the strangest thing you've ever made me do."

Morgan laughed. "I just wanted to see you wish upon a starfish." Lily shoved her playfully as they continued their walk.

As they were turning the corner back towards their apartment, Morgan's phone rang. Lily watched as she dug into her pocket to retrieve it. She studied the number for a moment before she placed the phone to her ear. "Hello?"

Patrick Wallace was a beloved man in Kennebunkport. Hundreds of people came to say their goodbyes. Lily hadn't realized how much he'd meant to Morgan until they'd come back for his funeral and she'd spoken on his behalf. When Lily heard Morgan talk about her grandfather, it brought back memories from her childhood.

"My grandfather loved the ocean. He used to say that it was the freest thing in the world. It defied all attempts to capture its essence with words. And as much as there were things to be said about it, there was much more that you couldn't. I like to think he was the same way. He loved Kennebunkport. He loved Maine. He loved his lighthouse. And he loved the ocean, with all its ebbs and flows. But he was too, a man that was outside the boundaries of definition. And that is how I'll always remember him. A man who was boundless."

After Morgan spoke, Lily read a poem by Henry Longfellow from her father's anthology. One whose page had been folded down so many times to mark it, that there'd been left a permanent crease.

My soul is full of longing,

For the secret of the sea,

And the heart of the great ocean,

Sends a thrilling pulse through me.

As he'd always wished, they scattered his ashes into the waters by the lighthouse, just as the sun was starting to set. As they were saying good-byes to those who had come to send Patrick Wallace off, a couple approached Morgan. Lily watched the woman as she wrapped her arms around her and pulled her into a hug. She looked as if she had been crying a long while.

"That was a beautiful tribute to Pat," her husband said. When Morgan was freed from the woman's grasp, the two shook her hand. "I'm Richard," he smiled at her and Lily. "This is Abigail. We live across the street."

Morgan wiped her eyes with the back of her hand, holding back tears. Lily reached out and shook their hands. "It's nice to meet you."

"Patrick wanted us to give this to you," Abigail said, handing Morgan an envelope. "If ever something happened to him. He said you'd know what to do with it."

Morgan studied the envelope for a long while before she opened it. Lily watched her eyes grow wider as she looked down the pages inside.

"What is it?" Lily asked her curiously.

"It's the deed to the lighthouse," Morgan said, breathlessly.

Later that evening, after everyone had left and the stars had started to spread across the skies, Lily and Morgan sat on the edge of the docks at the lighthouse, their feet dangling into the water. Neither of them had talked to one another much since the funeral. They'd been busy cleaning up after the wake. Finally, when they were alone, Lily looked to Morgan, a smile stretched across her face. Their hands clasped together softly.

"You want to know what I wished for?" Lily asked her. By the look on Morgan's face, she was taking a moment to figure out what Lily had meant by what she said. "On the starfish, I mean. I wished that we'd go where we were meant to go."

Morgan studied her for a moment, not speaking.

"This is where we were meant to go, Morgan," Lily said. "We're meant to come back home. You're meant to have your grandpa's lighthouse. Just like you always wanted."

When Lily Taylor returned to Seattle the next day, she went straight to the department store and bought the starfish photo. And she smiled and thought of Morgan Wallace the entire walk home.

Chapter Seven
Morgan

TIME SEEMED TO STAND still as Morgan and Lily pulled up to the hospital. As soon as Morgan was able to get Lily from the car and into her wheelchair, Lily raced through the parking lot. When Morgan looked up at the building, she found it hard to breathe. An ambulance horn sounded in the distance as it pulled up to the emergency room entrance and everything came crashing back to her in a terrifying wave of emotions.

Every time Morgan tried to take a step closer towards the building, she could hear her frantic screams into the stormy darkness. She could remember the terrifying feelings she felt, looking down from the rocks at the one person she loved most in the entire world mangled on the shores of the beach. The memories made it impossible to breathe. Morgan felt dizzy and forced herself to sit on the pavement, pushing her head between her legs.

When she heard the rattle of Lily's wheelchair across the pavement, she finally looked back up. "Morgan, are you okay?" As she reached her, Lily placed a hand on Morgan's shoulder.

"No, not really," Morgan said, taking another deep breath. It didn't take Lily but just a moment to realize what was going on. Morgan felt her squeeze her shoulder softly and the two of them met eyes at that moment.

"Everything is okay," Lily said, offering the best smile she could muster. "I'm here. I'm not going anywhere." Morgan let out a long sigh and shook her head. Then she got to her feet and wrapped her hands around the handlebars of Lily's wheelchair.

"Let's go," Morgan finally managed to say as she pushed her towards the entrance.

The waiting room of labor and delivery stirred up the same emotions in Morgan as the sight of the building had. She chose to keep them quiet, however, holding Lily's hand as they waited for any sign of John. They made casual conversation as they sat and Morgan could tell Lily was doing her best to distract her from her anxieties.

Two hours had passed when John finally appeared down the hallway. He looked exhausted, but a smile was stretched across his face. "Two healthy boys," John said as he sat down beside them, exhaling loudly. Lily's face lit up, laying her head on her brother's shoulder. John patted her on the top of her head, and the two interlaced their hands.

Morgan shared a glance with him and smiled. "How's Elise?"

"Good," John said. "The doctor said that her delivery couldn't have been any smoother."

"When can we see them?" Lily asked, and her brother sat up from the chair.

"Right now if you want."

Morgan and Lily followed at John's heel as they made their way down the long hallway to the delivery room. The white walls and fluorescent lights made Morgan sick to her stomach. It was all she could do to maintain her composure, but she forced herself to. For Lily. For her brother.

When they reached the door, John knocked before he entered. He stuck his head in the door first, speaking to Elise. "Can they come in and see the babies?" A moment later he opened the door, and Morgan pushed Lily inside the room. Elise lay on the bed, cradling two babies in her arms. They were wrapped snuggly in blankets, resting partly on her lap. She, like John, looked exhausted, but she was all smiles when she met eyes with Lily and Morgan.

Lily wandered over next to her, leaning over to look at the babies. Elise picked up one of the boys in her arms, cradling him. She handed him to Lily, who took him surprised. "Lily, meet Thomas." Morgan watched Lily's eyes light up when she looked at him, holding him close in her arms.

"Aren't you the most beautiful thing in the entire world," she said as she rocked him softly. Morgan couldn't help but watch her, captivated by her happiness and awe. While Lily sat with Thomas, Elise motioned for Morgan. She moved slowly to the side of the bed just as Elise scooped up the other baby and handed him to her. Morgan stepped back for a moment, slightly panicked.

"I'm not good with babies," she said, feeling rather awkward.

Elise smiled at her, still holding the infant out to her. "Well, you haven't held this baby." Morgan stared at him for a long time before she wrapped her hands around him, being careful to hold his head as she brought him to her chest. He looked up at her sleepily, barely able to keep his eyes open. Morgan felt feelings rush through her that she couldn't explain.

"Morgan, meet Ian," Elise said, and when the two met eyes, she smiled at her.

Morgan sat next to Lily, rocking Ian like Lily had been rocking Thomas. She couldn't keep her eyes off the baby, watching him so relaxed and calm in the blankets. Feeling his warm body bundled against her. Morgan didn't think she had ever seen something so perfect before in her life. She studied him for a long time. "Hello Ian," she finally whispered to him and for just a moment the two met eyes.

Finally, Morgan looked at Lily, watching her as she stared down at Thomas. When she looked up at Morgan, the two shared a smile with one another. Morgan couldn't help herself. She leaned in, planting her lips softly on Lily's. She let out a sigh when they met. "I love you," Morgan said when they parted, and she knew Lily's silent smile meant the same thing.

They held the babies for another minute before they carefully handed them back. As John and Elise cradled them, Morgan couldn't help but watch. For the first time in her life, Morgan longed for that feeling. That look of pure and perfect love that they shared when they looked at the marvelous humans they'd created.

Morgan looked back at Lily, watching her as she talked to her brother, beaming as brightly as she ever had. Watching how happy it made her, made Morgan all the happier. She'd never imagined in her life that she'd ever want children. Not until that moment.

After they'd spent a while with John and Elise, Morgan and Lily took a walk down the halls to look at the babies in the nursery. As they stared down into the glass window, Morgan looked down at Lily, watching her happy smile as she admired the newborns.

"You'd wanted to have one," Morgan finally said, putting a hand on her shoulder when she did. Lily looked up at her curiously. "A baby, I mean."

Lily smiled when their eyes met. "Were we thinking about having one?"

Again, the memory of the fight crossed her mind. She held it at bay, smiling back at Lily. Just as she was about to reply, John turned the corner, waving at them. "Elise wants to get a picture of us all together. Come on."

Lily stayed with her brother at the hospital that night, in spite of Morgan and John's reservations. The next day when Morgan awoke, she felt oddly alone without her. She got up a little earlier than normal to finish her chores. At seven, she arrived up the cracked pavement of her parent's driveway. She took a deep breath and hopped from the car, wandering up to the door.

Surprisingly, her mother answered. Her father had already headed off to work. He'd always been an early riser. It was partly where Morgan had gotten it from, as much as she refused to admit it. "Are you ready to go?" Morgan asked her, and her mother nodded, shutting and locking the house behind her. She argued with the door for a while trying to close it properly. It was so old it was crooked on its hinges. Morgan attempted to help, and eventually, it slammed shut.

"You should really get that replaced," Morgan said. The door, among a million other things that were in dire need of repair in their home.

"Oh, you know your father. We'll get by with it like this." Mary said as she turned towards her daughter. Morgan wanted so badly to argue with her, but she stayed quiet.

They went downtown to a greasy spoon diner they used to come to when she was a kid. She ordered her, and her mother pancakes to share and they each had a side of eggs and bacon. They made casual conversation for a while as they sipped coffee and watched the customers in the restaurant. Morgan could tell by the way that her mother was acting that she was forcing herself to stay in a positive mood.

"How has work been going?" Morgan finally asked her, and they shared a glance.

"Morgan, sweetheart, don't you worry about me." Mary gave her a small smile and reached out to hold her hand. "I can take care of myself."

"Has Dad talked to you about going to see a therapist?" Morgan asked her, even though she knew the answer.

Mary looked away from her and towards the table. "You know, your father and I talked about it. We thought it wasn't necessary after all. I'm going to do better about work, I promise."

Even though she was prepared for her answer, Morgan felt her face fall into her hand anyway. She sat there for a moment, trying to keep her composure. Finally, when she looked back at her mother, she spoke. "Mom, I don't care what *Dad* thinks you should do. I care about what *you* think you should do."

"And I told you, honey, I think I'm just fine."

Morgan met eyes with her again in disbelief. "Mom, you just told me the other day you can't even get out of bed some days. That's not just something you can shrug off. I know you and Dad think you can sweep everything under the rug, but you need to take care of yourself."

Mary didn't answer her. She sipped on her coffee and occasionally looked out the window beside the booth. Morgan finally grew sick of the silence and reached to take her mother's hand in her own again. "Mom, I really need you to listen to me okay? Can you look at me?"

As Morgan was about to speak, the waiter interrupted her with their food. After he'd left, her mother grew distracted with eating, and Morgan had lost track of her thought. They sat in silence while they ate. Morgan let her mother have most of the pancake. She wondered the last time that Paul and Mary had been out to eat anywhere. He was so stingy about money that even their home-cooked meals were always with cheap cuts of meat and vegetables that were on sale. Morgan doubted her mother had gotten a treat like this in a long while, if not the last time she and Morgan had gone out to breakfast together.

When they got back to her car and they'd both gotten inside, Morgan locked the doors on her mother and then hit the child lock. Mary stared for a moment, trying to realize what she'd done. Finally, her mother figured it out and turned to her, aggravated. "Morgan Wallace, did you just lock me in your car?"

"I did," Morgan replied sternly. "And I'm not going to let you out until you promise me that you'll let me take you to therapy."

Mary looked at her annoyed, fidgeting with the door handle. "I'm not a child, Morgan."

"I'm not saying you are. I'm saying, I need you to promise me that you'll let me take you to therapy. One session. I'll pay for everything. Just tell me you'll go."

Her mother stared out the window, a glaring look on her face. Neither of them spoke for a long while. Finally, when Mary turned to look at her, tears were rolling down her face. "You're father doesn't want me to go to therapy. He thinks it's a waste of money."

"I don't give a damn about what my father thinks," Morgan said, her voice raising slightly. When she noticed the tears in her mother's eyes, she calmed herself, reaching to put a hand on top of hers. "I need you to take care of yourself mom. I love you. I don't want something to happen to you."

"Nothing's going to happen to me, sweetheart," her mother said quietly.

"Promise me you'll let me take you to therapy," Morgan repeated herself. Mary met her eyes, and the two stared at each other. Morgan couldn't help but ache to see her mother look so sad.

"I promise," she finally said, and Morgan felt relief flow through her.

"Thank you," Morgan sighed, starting the car. Every inch of her filled with relief, as short-lived as it may have been.

Morgan stopped by the hardware store on the way home to pick up supplies. She spent the rest of the morning and part of the afternoon putting up a tile backsplash in the kitchen to match the new cabinet doors she and Lily had hung. The project took her mind off things, and when she'd finished, she couldn't help but be in a good mood. The house was really coming along.

When it drew close to dinner time, Morgan called Abigail and Richard to make sure they were still on for the evening. Then she got ready, finding herself in another pastel purple colored dress that she'd worn on one other occasion. As much as Morgan hated dressing up, it gave her a sort of thrill to see Lily's reaction when she did.

The minute that Morgan pulled into the driveway at John's, Lily raced out from the house in her wheelchair, rolling down the sidewalk. John followed behind her, giving a wave. As Morgan waved back, she watched Lily open the passenger side door and then situate herself to get inside. Impressively she did it all on her own.

John loaded the wheelchair into the back. He looked as exhausted as he had the previous day. "Don't keep her out too late," he joked before he shut the door. Once he had, he hopped in his car, and Morgan assumed he was off to head back to the hospital.

"I missed you all day," Lily said when they looked at one another. Morgan leaned over to kiss her softly on the lips. When they broke, they both were smiling. "You look amazing," she added, looking her over. Morgan smiled, that feeling she'd craved all afternoon washing over her. They kissed again, this time more deliberately. It wasn't till Morgan heard John's car honk at her that she finally backed out of the driveway.

Lily was in an excellent mood when they reached the restaurant in Portland. Abigail had done some hunting around to find a place where Lily could get in and out of without much help. Even though it had been last minute, they'd managed to get the last seats for the class that night. While Lily knew they were going to dinner, it wasn't until she saw the canvases that lined the tables that she realized.

"Did you bring me to Paint Night?" Lily asked Morgan as she wheeled her back to the corner seat. Richard and Abigail had beaten them there and had already made a space for her. Morgan smiled down at her as she took a seat.

"It was Abigail's idea," Morgan said, smiling at her across the table. Abigail and Richard had finished off a glass of wine and poured themselves and Lily and Morgan another. The two took sips of their drinks and settled in as the instructor began speaking.

While it wasn't a seascape, the picture of the tree in the field was peaceful to paint. Morgan watched Lily while she worked, focused and calm. In her element. Even when the class was nearly done, and Morgan had a half-finished painting, she would have paid for the class again just to watch Lily work.

"That was so much fun," Lily said when she'd finished her last detail on her picture. When she looked to Morgan, she laughed. "You didn't finish!"

"I know," Morgan smiled, and Lily switched out their paintings.

"Can I do it?" Lily asked, and Morgan nodded at her. Meanwhile, Abigail and Richard showed off their pieces while Morgan showed them Lily's.

"Always a natural," Richard said, admiring Lily's work. Abigail, Richard, and Morgan shared a lemon tart together while Lily sat engaged in painting again.

"Definitely not as good as your crust," Morgan noted when she took a bite.

"The secret is not to work the dough too much," Richard said as they finished it off. Just as they did, Lily looked up.

"Done!" She said, smiling. When Morgan looked at the painting, she couldn't believe it. Lily had made it into an entirely different picture. Instead of daytime, she'd made a night sky and painted streaks of moonlight across the field. Morgan was blown away at how detailed she'd gotten, even though this had been her first class since the accident.

"Lily, it's beautiful," Morgan exclaimed, holding it up for Richard and Abigail to see. Even they seemed in awe of how detailed and precise she'd been. Morgan wondered for a minute if maybe she'd somehow remembered some of what she'd learned before.

It seemed as if Lily had the same idea. "I felt like I already knew what I was doing. That's the first time I've felt that way." Lily pondered for a moment. "Do you think I remembered it? From before?"

Morgan didn't know for sure, but the idea that she had made her overwhelmed with emotion. That there was a tiny piece of her from before that had been preserved. All she could do was smile at her, and when she did, Lily wrapped her hands around her face and kissed her, deeply.

THE EVENING THAT JOHN and Elise brought the twins home from the hospital, Lily and Morgan spent cleaning the house and preparing the nursery. When they arrived, Morgan and Lily helped get them all situated before they decided to take their leave. At the lighthouse, just as they'd finished fixing dinner together, Lily looked out the kitchen window at the skies. It was a beautiful starry night out, not a cloud to be seen.

"Let's have our dock picnic," Lily suggested. While Lily packed up the food, Morgan brought pillows and blankets out to the dock to make sure Lily was comfortable. The full moon shined brightly above her while she worked. When she finally came to fetch Lily, she'd wrapped up two plates and cradled them in her arms with a bottle of wine as Morgan toted her outside.

"Are you sure you're going to be comfortable?" Morgan asked Lily once she'd set her down amongst the pillows and blankets

"It's perfect," Lily said, smiling at her. The two unpackaged their food and sat side by side, looking out at the ocean as they ate and drank. Morgan felt herself lulled by the soothing sound of the waves as they hit the shore. When they finally finished their food, Lily took her plate from her and sat it behind them. Morgan wrapped her in the blanket and pulled her close.

"Are you still feeling okay?" Morgan asked her, and Lily looked up to meet her eyes. She nodded and then stared back at the ocean.

"I was remembering going swimming here when we were kids," Lily said thoughtfully. "We used to play till we were so tired we'd collapse on the dock." The two of them smiled reflecting on the memory. When they met eyes again, Morgan reached to stroke Lily's cheek softly with her thumb.

"That's not my favorite memory," Morgan admitted, and when Lily looked at her curiously, she continued. "Let's just say picnics aren't the only thing this dock and that ocean are good for."

Morgan watched Lily smile and think about the idea again for a moment. Suddenly her face grew somber. "I hope I can swim again," she said quietly, turning her attention back to the water. Neither of them spoke for a while, Morgan ran her hand up and down Lily while she held her. Finally, Morgan unraveled herself. When she did, she stood up and pulled the clothes from her body in fluid motions until she stood naked, her skin glowing softly under the light of the moon. Lily watched her curiously as Morgan came to meet her, pulling the clothes off her body.

"What are you doing?" Lily whispered, slightly embarrassed. "Someone could see us."

Morgan didn't give her any mind, scooping her off of the ground and cradling her close. She made her way down off the dock and onto the sandy patch of beach that lined either side. For a moment Morgan watched the ocean waves roll in and out slowly. Then she made careful steps into the water. The water was chillier than she expected but still tolerable.

Lily giggled as the mist from the water hit her. Morgan stepped off the small bank into the deeper part. It quickly came up to her chest, surrounding her and Lily.

"It's cold!" Lily squeaked, clinging on to Morgan's neck. They circled around for a minute or so before they adjusted and the water started to feel relaxing. Lily loosened her grip on Morgan, letting one of her hands wade the water. When Morgan watched her, she could see her bright smile spread across her face.

"I can't remember the last time I was in the water," she said breathlessly, watching the motions of her hands as they made ripples. The small waves rocked against them as Morgan carried her around. Finally, Morgan paused, and the two of them met eyes.

"Do you want to try to stand?" Morgan asked her, curiously.

"Is that a good idea?" Lily asked.

"I'll hold you up. It might be nice to stretch your legs."

Lily hesitated for a moment before she nodded. Morgan leaned her down carefully wrapping her hand around Lily's waist as she released her legs. As promised, Morgan held her, so she lightly put weight on her legs. They moved slowly in the water, so Lily could feel the sand beneath her toes. It sent such intense waves of happiness through Morgan to see Lily so content that she could barely breathe. Finally, Lily leaned into Morgan and let her cradle her in her arms once more.

When Lily finally looked back to Morgan, they stared at each other under the pale glowing light of the moon. Morgan could see the reflection of the water casting off her grey eyes. Lily placed her hand against Morgan's cheek, and their two mouths met.

Morgan brought Lily to the dock and reached down for a blanket, wrapping them both in it. They laid down against the pillows, their lips meeting over and over.

"Want to go inside?" Morgan asked her when they finally took a breath. She rolled her hand down Lily's naked flesh, running her fingers across her breasts and down the length of her stomach. It made goosebumps on her skin. Lily shook her head, looking up into Morgan's eyes before they kissed again, deeply. Just as Morgan's lips began to trail down Lily's soft skin, she felt her fingers reach on the side of her face. Morgan looked up at her, and they stared quietly at each other for a moment.

"I love you," Lily whispered to her, and it filled Morgan with a burning fire she could not contain. Morgan took her time, leaving no part untouched. Pleasuring every part of Lily until she was gasping for air, begging for release. Finally, her soft cries filled the night as they came together, a tangled mess of bodies.

The Lighthouse

THE FIRST TIME MORGAN Wallace spent the night in the lighthouse with Lily Taylor, she knew it was meant to be. They'd arrived with the moving truck in the early evening, in the midst of a torrential downpour. Morgan had insisted waiting until morning to get the boxes from the truck, but Lily had dug out one item from the back before they made their way inside.

In a box nestled under the stairs of the lighthouse, Morgan found an old toolkit of Patrick Wallace's. She watched as Lily carefully hung the picture of the starfish next to the front door, while Morgan wrapped her arms around her, pressing their bodies close together. She brushed the hair from her neck, planting kisses into her skin. As soon as Lily had finished, she turned, the two meeting in a passionate embrace.

"Welcome home," Lily said with a smile when they parted. She brushed a piece of Morgan's damp curls from her face. Morgan couldn't help but smile back, pressing their lips together once more.

It didn't take long before sopping wet pieces of clothing began to hit the floor. When there was nothing but skin between them, Morgan pressed Lily up against the wall, their bodies woven tightly together.

"You know what I think," Morgan whispered into Lily's ear before she kissed it softly. Lily sighed, pressing back into Morgan as her hands wrapped around her body. "I think we need to break this place in. What do you think?"

Lily didn't have to think anything. They came together, Morgan running her hands over Lily's naked flesh until she was gasping for air. They moved through the empty house, filling every room with their cries of ecstasy. When they finished, Lily made peanut butter and jelly sandwiches while Morgan spread blankets and pillows along the living room floor. They sat against the wall, finishing off their food while they listened to the soft pattering of the rain as it hit the roof.

As they laid on the floor, nestled together underneath piles of sheets, Lily shared her ideas for decorating the house. Morgan listened quietly, holding her close and breathing in her subtle scent. After a while, Lily turned to look at her, her fingers lightly grazing Morgan's cheek.

"Are you listening?" Lily whispered with a smile.

"Every word," Morgan said, kissing her softly on the nose. Her lips trailed down to meet Lily's, and they breathed each other in for a moment. It wasn't long before they found themselves lost in one another all over again.

That night Morgan Wallace realized that she didn't need Lily Taylor's starfish. For the first time in her life, she had everything she'd ever wanted.

Chapter Eight
Lily

IT WAS A BRIGHT SUNNY day in the middle of fall. The trees had just started to change colors. John had invited the family over to enjoy the last warm days of grilling out before the chilly fall air settled in. Morgan and Lily had arrived early toting a salad and wine.

Lily made her way carefully through the house. By now she'd gotten used to not having to look at her feet when she walked. Instead, she noticed the placement of the cane that supported her body weight on her left side. As she walked into the kitchen, she could feel her brother's prying eyes as she helped Morgan open the fridge to put the salad away.

"I'm okay," Lily turned towards him, offering a small smile. "Still getting used to it."

"You're doing great," John said, pleased. Lily took a seat at the table as Elise came to bring glasses of wine. Morgan thanked her graciously.

"Carmela thinks I'll only need the cane for another month or two," Lily said, stretching her legs out under the table. Morgan reached for her hand and cupped it gently in her own, stroking the backside with her thumb.

Elise had dressed up the twins in matching outfits. Morgan and Lily played with them while her sister-in-law and John finished up making the food. Lily couldn't believe how fast they'd grown over the past two months.

"I want one," Lily said to Morgan as Ian sat in her lap. The two exchanged glances for a moment. Lily couldn't read the expression on

Morgan's face, but they were quickly distracted by plates of delicious food put in front of them.

While Elise and Morgan cleaned up dinner afterward, Lily and her brother sat out on the swing in the backyard, watching the sun disappear behind the trees. They were quiet for a while, enjoying each other's company. Finally, Lily could feel her brother's eyes staring into her cheek.

"Are you ready for work tomorrow?" John asked her curiously.

Lily turned to meet his glance. "I think so." After much deliberation, Lily had finally agreed to go back to the research center. Ryan had offered to take her out on the boat and get her up to speed on the projects they were working on.

"Just take it easy," John said patting her softly on the back. "Don't overextend yourself."

Lily shook her head, smiling at him. "I don't know why you worry so much. I'm fine."

When they looked at each other again, Lily noticed the somewhat solemn look in her brother's eyes. "I don't want anything to happen to you." It was the way he said it that made Lily realize what he meant. She took his hand softly into her own and squeezed it.

"I'm not going anywhere."

"I'm really proud of you, you know," John said, wiping his face with the back of his hand. "I'm sure they'd be proud of you too."

Lily could feel a tug in her chest for a moment. They sat in silence again before Elise came out onto the back porch to get them.

"Who's ready for dessert?"

The following morning, Lily woke before Morgan. A rush of nervous energy filled her as she stared into the darkness. Finally, she pulled herself from the bed quietly, making her way down into the hall. She'd grown accustomed to waking early now and found herself enjoying the quiet hours of chores with Morgan.

As she worked to raise the flag on her own, she felt a gentle embrace from behind her. Morgan rested her chin on Lily's shoulder as she tied off the rope and then turned to face her. Their lips met briefly and when they parted Morgan smiled at her.

"I think that's a first," Morgan said as they made their way back into the house. "I don't think you've ever beaten me up." Lily smiled at her as they made their way across the house to the doors of the lighthouse.

"I'm a little wound up," Lily admitted.

The two finished the chores for the morning and spent the early hours watching the sunrise from the top of the lighthouse. After Lily got ready, the two loaded up into the car and made their way to Portland. Most of the ride was spent in silence, Lily lost in thought about what the day might bring and bundled with nerves. When Morgan pulled into the research park, Lily found herself starting to lose her nerve. That was until she saw her co-workers standing next to a beautiful boat on the docks.

Morgan and Lily made their way down to greet Ryan, who was loading some equipment. When they reached him, he gave a smile. "Glad to see you could make it," he said, extending his hand. Lily took it graciously and smiled back at him.

"Do you need any help?" Lily asked as he set another box on the floor of the boat.

Ryan shook his head. "You can hop in, we'll take off here in a few."

Lily let Morgan assist her into the boat and sat down beside two interns who introduced themselves. As the boat rocked gently back and forth, Lily could feel her heart start to race in her chest. Morgan took a step away from her and Lily reached out and grasped her wrist. The two met eyes and Morgan looked down at her slightly concerned.

"Are you okay?"

Lily took a few long deep breaths and nodded. "Yeah," she shook her head. "Yeah, I'm fine."

When Morgan looked convinced, she leaned down and gently kissed her on the lips. "Have a good time. I'll be by to pick you up in a few hours."

Lily nodded and watched as she exited the boat and headed back down the dock. Just as she did, Ryan loaded the last of the equipment and stepped inside. "Alright kids, let's get this show on the road." He clapped his hands together and sat down at the helm, studying over the boat. After a minute, Lily felt it begin to back away from the dock.

As she watched the shore grow further and further away, her heart began to race again. She could feel every movement of the boat. Every wave that hit the side. Blood was running so hard through her body that she could hear it thumping in her head.

"We're just going to go around the harbor a bit and check out our first feeding site," Ryan explained to Lily. She did her best to nod, even though she could hardly hear him. The further away they got, the worse the feelings got. It wasn't long before Lily felt unable to breathe.

A wave crashed into the boat and Lily folded her body over her legs, her breath in shallow pants. Ryan came to sit beside her, and she could feel his hand resting on her back.

"Lily, are you okay?" It was impossible for her to answer. She could barely stay coherent her heart was racing so fast.

"I can't breathe," Lily gasped, trying to steady herself. "I can't breathe."

Lily heard Ryan call out to an intern, who took his place while Ryan returned to the helm. The boat raced back in the opposite direction, and as it did, Lily felt herself fade in and out of consciousness.

The next thing she recalled was laying against the dock, staring up at the skies. Morgan, Ryan, and Bill all hovered above her. When she was able to sit up, Ryan offered her a drink of water while Morgan gently stroked her back.

"Are you alright?" Morgan asked her, a look of concern spread across her face. Lily nodded, taking long deep breaths. Her heart had returned to normal, and she felt as if she could breathe again.

"I couldn't breathe," Lily said, placing a hand on her forehead. "I don't know what happened."

"I think you had a panic attack," Ryan said as she handed him back the water. "Do you think you can stand up?"

Lily nodded and used Morgan to help stand herself up. Once she had, Bill handed her cane and the three of them walked down the docks. Suddenly a wave of embarrassment flooded over Lily.

"I'm really sorry," she said, looking to Ryan. Ryan gave her a wave and smiled.

When Morgan and Lily got back into the car, Lily let out a long exasperated sigh, staring out the window. Morgan reached over to carefully take her hand in her own and squeezed it. "It was your first time back on a boat."

"I don't know how it bothered me, I can't even remember the accident."

"Maybe you remember some of it subconsciously," Morgan said as they pulled out of the parking lot. "Who knows how it works."

By the time they'd gotten back to the lighthouse, Lily had returned back to nearly normal. They made dinner, and then the two finished putting up the new curtains around the house. The place looked almost like an entirely different home, most of the renovations having been completed. When they finished, they laid stretched out on the couch, Lily's head in Morgan's lap while they watched television.

"Do you ever think about moving?" Lily asked, stroking down the length of Morgan's arm. Morgan caught glances with her and seemed to ponder the question for a while.

"Sometimes," Morgan said finally, offering a small smile. "I feel like it's starting to feel like home here though, don't you think?" Her fingers ran through Lily's hair softly.

Lily looked around the room, admiring all the hard work that had gone into the past few months. It was nearly finished now. Everything from the lighting fixtures to the hardwood floor had been redone.

"It's really nice," Lily agreed. "I just was thinking about if we ever wanted to start a family. We'd need a bigger place, don't you think?"

Morgan suddenly looked distant, her hand pausing. "Maybe."

The conversation went quiet after that, and the two resumed watching television. All the while Lily couldn't help but wonder if Morgan felt the same way, or if she'd ever want to leave the lighthouse at all.

Early the next morning, Lily, Morgan, and John made another trip to Portland to see Dr. Matthew's at Southern Maine. It had been nearly a month since Lily's last visit, and the first time since her hospital stay she'd had an MRI. Anxiety filled the car as they drove. John sang off-key with the radio periodically, mostly as a way to distract them all since he'd never been much of a singer.

When they arrived at the hospital, Lily walked inside on her own, feeling Morgan and her brother's prying eyes as she went. Even after all this time, they still worried something might happen to her.

The visit took most of the morning, with the MRI and bloodwork and a million questions from nurses. Lily was filled with so much anxiety she thought she might burst. Finally, Dr. Matthews arrived, and she could tell by the look on his face that she wasn't going to like the news he had to offer.

He sat down in his chair across from Lily. Morgan had her hand wrapped tightly around Lily's while John rested against the wall, his arms crossed over his chest. Dr. Matthews offered them all a small smile as his eyes wandered over Lily's chart.

"We've taken a look at your MRI scans, and I spoke with your physical therapist earlier today. You've been doing really well," Dr. Matthews met eyes with Lily.

"Just tell me," Lily begged him, feeling her leg shake as she waited.

"I'm afraid that your scans show a significant amount of scarring around the area we repaired," Dr. Matthew's said, looking at them all.

"Which means?" John asked.

"Lily," Dr. Matthews said, his voice calm and eyes staring directly into hers. "I don't think you will regain any more function in your legs."

Lily sat for a moment, trying to understand what he'd said. "I'm still in physical therapy. You said I've been doing really good."

"There's just too much scarring," Dr. Matthew's explained. "I'm afraid that even with more therapy, you aren't going to see much more improvement than you've already had."

The longer Lily sat contemplating his words, the greater the ringing in her ears became. Suddenly, even though Dr. Matthew's had been speaking, she couldn't hear what he was saying over the loudness of it. She watched as he turned to speak to Morgan and John, who both looked as devastated as Lily did.

"So you're saying I'll have to walk with a cane for the rest of my life?" Lily asked, still in disbelief. Dr. Matthew's nodded. Lily found her entire body shaking.

"I'm so sorry," he said calmly. All Lily could do was sit in silence, trying to force herself to breathe. She felt the gentle touch of John's hand running up and down her back. Morgan had not let go of her the entire time.

Lily was silent the entire ride home. When John had asked if she wanted to stop for a bite to eat, she told them no. There was no argument. They drove straight home, silence filling the car. When they reached the lighthouse, Lily got out quietly and walked into the house while Morgan and her brother spoke. She collapsed on the bed in a heap, throwing her cane against the floor.

Once she'd settled, Morgan came to check on her. She sat on the edge of the bed, running her hand along Lily's arm. "Are you okay?"

"No," Lily managed to say, hoarsely. "No, I'm not."

Morgan sat with her a while until Lily found herself falling asleep. She didn't leave the bed for the entire rest of the day. When Morgan finally came to lay down, she was wide awake, staring up at the ceiling.

"Do you want to talk about it?" Morgan asked when she'd laid down beside her.

Lily turned to look at her, tears streaming down her face. Morgan wiped at them gently with her thumb, giving her a small smile. "Oh, Lily." Lily leaned into her, burying her face in her chest and sobbing loudly. She cried for a while, and Morgan let her. When she finally recovered the two looked at each other again.

"I just need to be by myself for a little while," Lily admitted, and Morgan nodded, brushing a strand of hair from her face. "I'm sorry, Morgan."

"Don't be sorry," Morgan leaned over to kiss her on the cheek. "I'll be on the couch if you need me." She ran her fingers across the top of Lily's head for a moment before she stood up and took her leave.

The next morning, Lily slept in for a while until she smelled breakfast. Finally, she roused herself out of bed, finding Morgan busy in the kitchen. The room was filled with the aroma of bacon and toast. As soon as Lily found her way to the table, Morgan sat a plate in front of her, smiling softly.

"Did you sleep okay?" Morgan asked, and Lily nodded, taking a bite of toast.

"You didn't have to sleep on the couch all night," Lily noted when the two met eyes. Morgan shrugged and waved it off. She turned back to the stove, finishing off the rest of the food and plating some for herself. When she returned to the table, she sat a cup of coffee in front of Lily and then sat beside her.

Something about her felt off. Lily looked at her curiously as they ate. "You're always so nice to me." After taking another bite of food, Morgan looked up.

"It's no big deal. It's just breakfast."

"No," Lily said, shaking her head. "About everything. You always go above and beyond. Like you're trying too hard." For a second, Morgan looked offended. Lily was quick to take her hand in hers. "Don't get me wrong. I appreciate it. It just feels off. I don't know. Maybe I'm crazy."

"Where is this coming from?" Morgan asked, wiping her face with her napkin. "Are you sure you're okay?"

"I'm fine. It's you I'm worried about," Lily admitted, taking a sip of coffee.

The two sat in silence for a minute, eating their food and pondering what Lily had said. Finally, Morgan turned her attention back to Lily.

"There's something I need to tell you," Morgan finally admitted, and Lily felt a wave of relief overcome her. She wasn't crazy after all. "I've meant to tell you for a while now, but after everything that happened yesterday.." Morgan trailed off for a moment before she returned her attention back to what she was saying. "I never told you what happened that night of the accident."

Lily looked curiously at her. "It's fine Morgan, I don't remember anything. It doesn't matter anymore."

"It matters to me," Morgan said, and for the first time, Lily noticed guilt on her face. "Because I feel like it was my fault it happened." Lily couldn't quite piece together what she had meant, so Morgan continued. "We'd been having some problems for a while. Differences in opinions about things."

"What kind of differences?" Lily asked, sitting back in her chair.

"You'd wanted to move and start a family," Morgan admitted. "And I wasn't ready. You wanted to sell the lighthouse, and I didn't. Those sorts of differences." Lily didn't know what to say, so she nodded instead. "You asked me to marry you, and I turned you down."

The expression on Lily's face turned surprised. "I asked you to marry me?" Morgan nodded in reply.

"I think after that night, it was the cause of all of our problems. And we had a fight again, the night of your accident. About the lighthouse. And I've felt like it was my fault ever since." Morgan took a deep and shaky breath, placing a hand over her mouth to stifle a cry. "And I'm so sorry."

Lily reached for Morgan's hand again, holding it in her own. She smiled softly. "You don't need to be sorry. It wasn't your fault." Morgan nodded, wiping her face with the back of her hand. "There's no sense in blaming yourself for things like that. You shouldn't have to carry that burden." Morgan sighed when she said it. Lily embraced her, holding her tightly.

"Besides," Lily continued when they'd parted. "I feel better about it now that I've had some time to think about it. It's going to be okay. I can live with this. We can have those things now. It's different than it was before."

Morgan took their plates to the sink to wash them. As she worked, Lily moved to stand beside her. "Right? It's different now?" When Morgan didn't answer at first, Lily felt her heart sink into her chest.

"Of course it's different," Morgan said, turning to look at her after she'd handed Lily a plate to dry. "Everything changed after the accident. It doesn't mean I don't feel the same way about the lighthouse. About getting married."

"What do you mean? Are you saying you won't?" Lily finished the dish and set it in the cabinet just as Morgan handed her the second.

When Morgan didn't answer her, Lily turned, feeling somewhat offended. "You're saying you won't."

"Not yet," Morgan said, turning to look at her. "I don't know when. I don't know if I can, Lily."

"Even after everything we've been through?" Lily felt a sadness wash over her. "You won't even consider it?"

"Why can't you just be okay staying here? I've bent over backward to make this place better for you. I don't understand why you hate the lighthouse so much."

"I don't hate the lighthouse," Lily said, frustrated. "I don't understand why you're so afraid of taking another step. Even after everything that has happened. No wonder you feel guilty. You feel guilty because you haven't changed."

Morgan looked angry then, shutting the cabinet door and turning away from her for a moment. Lily stared at the back of her head intensely until she turned back around. When they met eyes, Lily knew that nothing was going to change her mind.

"Morgan, I don't think I can be in a relationship that is going to go nowhere," Lily finally said, feeling her heart sink into her chest when she realized it. "Especially after all of this has happened. Maybe you were right for telling me about everything. Maybe it was good we dealt with this now, instead of letting it go on."

"Are you serious?" Morgan stared at her, her expression unreadable.

"You don't want to get married? Start a life together?"

"We have a life together!" Morgan snapped, slamming her hand on the countertop. "I don't like you forcing ultimatums on me. You did this before, you're doing it again now. I can't help the way that I feel. You need to understand that."

"I can't help the way that I feel either," Lily said calmly. The two stared at one another, unable to come up with the words to say. Finally Lily cleared her throat. "I think it might be best if I stay with John for a while."

Morgan stewed, not speaking. When she finally cleared her throat, she nodded. Lily gathered some of her things and waited by the door for her brother.

While she sat, Morgan came over to sit beside her. "Don't you think we should try and talk about this?"

Lily exchanged a glance with her. "Is it going to change your mind?"

Morgan paused for a moment before she shook her head.

"I think we need time to figure things out," Lily replied, feeling a sadness wash over her.

When John finally arrived, Morgan walked her to the car. They barely spoke, hugging each other briefly. Lily felt every piece of her breaking inside when she shut the car door, and her brother took off down the road. In the side mirror, Lily watched Morgan standing in the driveway until she disappeared from sight.

The Snowstorm

FROM THE MOMENT MORGAN Wallace got snowed in with Lily Taylor, she knew they'd be together for the rest of their lives. The door slammed behind Morgan as she rushed back into the house. Snow littered the ground around her. She shook the remnants from her hair, shivering as she made her way up the staircase. As she shed herself of her winter clothes, Lily handed her a cup of hot chocolate. It smelled divine.

"They said at least another foot," Lily said as they sat on the couch next to each other. When Morgan turned to look out the window, snow was already piled up underneath the pane outside. "We're going to be stuck in here for days," Lily said, playfully smirking at her. "Whatever are we going to do?"

"Oh, I have plenty to do with you," Morgan replied, wrapping her in her arms. Lily giggled as the two fell on the couch together.

Later that evening, naked and bundled in blankets, Lily's head lay in Morgan's lap as they watched an old movie together that the two had seen at least a hundred times. Occasionally Morgan would interject lines in such a way that it sent Lily into fits of laughter

Finally, the two met eyes and Morgan ran her fingers over the top of Lily's head. They stared at each other for a moment before Lily sighed softly.

"What is it?" Lily asked, and Morgan realized she must have been lost in thought.

"Oh, nothing," she admitted. "I just can't believe this, is all."

"Can't believe what?" Lily asked, sitting up to look at her properly.

Morgan studied her a moment, stroking her fingers along the side of Lily's face. Tracing the edges. They met briefly in a kiss, and when Morgan pulled away, she smiled. "That you're here with me. That this is real. I keep thinking what my high school self would say if she knew that one day Lily Taylor would be lying naked. In the house they lived in together. In the middle of a snowstorm."

Lily laughed, taking Morgan's hands into her own. "You know what's funny," she said, offering a smile. Morgan felt her fingers stroke her skin and it sent butterflies through her. "I think I knew all along."

"Knew what?" Morgan echoed.

"That we'd be together. Someday, anyway."

The two sat in silence for a moment before Morgan pulled them together, wrapping her tightly in an embrace. "I want to stay like this forever," she whispered, kissing her on the side of the neck.

"Me too," Lily sighed, running her fingers down Morgan's back. Morgan leaned back to look at her for a moment, the two bundled together in the blankets. When she did, she realized something that hadn't occurred to her until that very moment. Morgan Wallace knew without a shadow of a doubt that she wanted to spend the rest of her life with Lily Taylor. And she wasn't afraid of the idea. Not in the very least.

Chapter Nine
Morgan

"THAT'LL BE A HUNDRED and sixty-four fifty," the woman at the cash register said. Morgan handed over the money and took her change, toting out a cart-full of supplies. It had been an entire week since Lily and Morgan last spoke. The first few days had been painful. Morgan called every day, desperately wanting to talk to her, to no avail. John would answer, fighting her tooth and nail every time. Eventually, after a few days, she gave up the fight and decided to occupy her time elsewhere.

Morgan had figured, if she fixed up the lighthouse enough, Lily was bound to come around. The stupid fight would end, and she'd come back. So she consumed her time in house chores and repairs.

When she got back to the lighthouse that afternoon, tourists were waiting. After she'd given them a quick look around, she resumed the task of replacing the baseboards and fixing the crown molding around the house. It took her well into the evening and most of the following day to get through.

The next Saturday, Abigail, and Richard dropped by in the afternoon to help with painting. Morgan treated them to beers, and they made a time of it. She'd spent ages at the store, struggling over which colors would best work. Eventually, she had an employee help her decide, praying that Lily would like it when she saw it. When they got Abigail's approval, Morgan felt better about it. After the three of them finished painting, they enjoyed a freshly cooked meal out on the porch together, admiring the sunset.

"For amateur painters, I say we did a pretty good job," Richard said, holding up his beer. Morgan and Abigail clinked their glasses with his, nodding in agreement.

"Have you talked to Lily?" Abigail asked after she took a drink of wine. The three of them had worked on a buzz the entire afternoon, and Morgan was still feeling it. When Morgan shook her head, she could see the disappointed look in Abigail's eyes.

"She doesn't want to talk to me," Morgan explained. "I've tried a hundred times, and she won't listen to what I have to say." Her voice came out in a huff. When Abigail looked at her curiously, Morgan decided to explain the situation at length. By the end of it, she couldn't tell if they approved or disapproved of her decisions, so she sat quietly waiting.

Finally, Abigail spoke again, smiling softly. "Marriage is a complicated thing." For a moment Morgan thought that would be all she would say, but then she continued. "Richard didn't want to get married."

Morgan looked at Richard, and he nodded. "Just not a traditionalist." It was as if he'd taken the words straight from Morgan's mouth. "My parents had a bad marriage. Never understood the point."

"So why did you get married then?" Morgan asked him, taking another drink of beer.

"Because I loved Abigail more than I loved the idea of not getting married," Richard said simply. It took Morgan aback. She didn't know how to respond, so instead, she sat there, letting it sink in.

After they'd finished their meals, Abigail and Richard helped Morgan clean up the food and the painting supplies before they took their leave. When she was alone, Morgan couldn't help but be troubled by her thoughts. Wondering if she was making the right decision in regards to Lily. If she shouldn't just give in. Yet a part of her still couldn't shake the thought that Lily could compromise too. Finally, with a mind drowned in liquor, Morgan found herself drifting off to sleep on the couch.

The next morning she was awoken abruptly by the sound of a phone call. Even amidst a hangover, Morgan rushed to grab it, hoping that it was Lily. She was disappointed to find that it wasn't.

"Mom?"

An hour later, Morgan arrived a mess at her parents home. It was a wonder she had forced herself to come given the state of her head and her impatience given her present circumstances. When her father opened the door, she could tell by his demeanor that he was even more hungover than she was. "Where is she?" Morgan asked when he stood in the doorway. When he pointed to the bathroom, she went to the door and knocked.

"Are you okay in there?" Morgan could hear her mother heaving on the other side of the door. She opened it quickly, rushing to her aid. The two sat in the bathroom for a while until Mary settled. Morgan could smell the alcohol from across the room.

"Had a little too much to drink last night?" Morgan asked, running her fingers through her hair. When her mother shook her head, Morgan laughed. "Mom, you reek. You can't lie about it."

Embarrassed, Mary pulled herself off of the floor, running water over her face. "I just had a rough day yesterday," she admitted. "And then your father and I got into this silly argument.." Morgan let her ramble on for a moment.

"Did you go to therapy on Monday?" She asked when her mother finished speaking. When Mary couldn't look her in the eyes, Morgan knew the answer to that question was something she didn't want to hear. "Oh, Mom, are you serious? Did you go last week?" Again, when she gave no response, Morgan's heart sunk deeper into her chest.

"You need to talk to someone," Morgan said, looking genuinely concerned.

"I'm fine, Morgan, honestly," Mary shook her head, weaving around her daughter and out into the living room. Morgan's father was waiting on the couch, nursing his head.

It wasn't clear whether it was those exact words, the hangover, the massive amount of stress she was under, or a combination of the three, but Morgan snapped. "I'm done," she said flatly, her eyes drifting between her parents. "I can't do this anymore."

"What do you mean, 'you can't do this anymore?'" Her father stared at her with his arms crossed over his chest.

"You two have been consuming my life for years," Morgan said, placing the back of her hand on her head. "I've been bending over backward to help you, and it's like you don't want to be helped."

Mary looked at her. "Sweetheart, we can take care of ourselves just fine."

Morgan sighed, turning to look at her. "And that's fine. If you want to take care of yourself, then do it. Leave me out of it. When you want to go to therapy and take your life seriously, you can call me. But until then, I need you to stop. I can't take this anymore."

Before they could say much else, Morgan left in haste, charging towards her car. As she moved across the yard, she could hear her father following at her heel.

"How dare you treat your mother that way," he snapped at her and Morgan turned swiftly to meet him.

"Dad, you need to grow the hell up," she said, staring him down. "Man up and take care of your wife for once in your damn life. She needs you." Morgan's father stared at her, not speaking. "I'm tired of doing your job for you. It's not my responsibility. So you two need to figure it out. And until you do, I'm done. I can't do this anymore."

Paul stood quietly, glaring at her as she hopped into the car and pulled out of the driveway. Morgan felt on fire as she left, but it was a good fire. A kind of fire she hadn't felt in a very long time. Her heart raced nearly the entire drive. When she finally pulled into the driveway of the lighthouse, she had made up her mind.

The entire afternoon, Morgan spent drafting out the final details to finish the lighthouse. While it was closer to being fixed up than it had ever been, there was still some work yet to be done. As soon as she had plans, she trekked over to Abigail and Richards. Abigail was busy trimming bushes in the front of the yard.

"I need your help," Morgan said, showing her the notes she'd made. "How long is this going to take me to finish?"

"Let's get Richard," Abigail replied, showing her inside.

"I think you could get this done in two weeks," Richard said, sipping a cup of coffee while he mulled over Morgan's papers. "Maybe three, unless you really push it. We'll help with what we can."

"Thanks," Morgan said smiling.

Just as Morgan set to leave, she caught Abigail as they headed out.

"Your sister Barbara," Morgan said, catching her glance. "You said she was a real estate agent in town, right?" Abigail nodded, standing in the doorway. Morgan smiled. "Any chance I could get her number?"

The next morning, Barbara showed up at the lighthouse only an hour after Morgan had called her. She looked absolutely thrilled when she wandered inside. "Well isn't this place quite the charmer!"

While they wandered around, Morgan felt her heart racing in her chest listening as Barbara rattled off the necessary steps that had to be done. Morgan explained some of the last repairs she planned to do in the next few weeks, and it seemed to bode well.

"Now I'm sure you're wondering what this kind of place will go for," Barbara said when they'd sat down at the kitchen table. It had been the only thing on Morgan's mind since she'd arrived. "It's going to be a bit tricky, seeing as it's such a historic place. We may even be able to get the city to buy it from you. I did a bit of research and came up with some numbers." Barbara slid a paper across the table to her and Morgan scanned down it quietly. All of the estimates were more than enough to cover what she needed.

"How soon can we put it up for sale?" Morgan asked.

"Immediately, if you're ready."

While Morgan had never been more terrified in her life, she also knew without a shadow of a doubt that she most certainly was ready. The two worked on paperwork throughout the morning. When they'd finished, Morgan made them both some coffee and they sat and chatted a little while longer. As Barbara was about to take her leave, Morgan stopped her.

"I have one more favor to ask."

TWO WEEKS LATER, ABIGAIL and Richard were over in the early evening to help fix a new front door to the house. Morgan had worked herself to the bone getting all the repairs done promptly. The door was the final chore that needed to be completed, and it felt like a befitting one. As they locked it in place, the three of them stood back to admire their handiwork. It was a beautiful red door that looked perfect with the blue and white exterior of the lighthouse. Lily had always wanted a red door, but Morgan had thought it was tacky. Once again, Lily had proved her wrong.

"How does it feel to have everything done?" Abigail asked as the three of them sat down on the porch together.

"Surreal," Morgan admitted, enjoying the cool evening air. She could hear the wind whipping at the flag above them and looked up at it for a moment. As she did, a pair of headlights flashed as a car pulled into the driveway. Morgan recognized it the second she saw it.

"Hello, hello!" Barbara said as she hopped out of the car, wielding a stack of papers. She wandered over to the three, beaming. "I have some fantastic news!" Morgan didn't even have to ask. "You've got yourself another buyer!" A few days before, Morgan had gotten an offer from a woman who had wanted to turn the place into a bed and breakfast. She'd made a great offer, and everything had been good to go. Then suddenly, without warning, it had fallen through.

The words filled Morgan with a slew of emotions. Mostly though, she was relieved. "Really?"

Barbara couldn't stop smiling. "They offered over the asking price, and they're paying in cash!" Morgan could hardly believe it. "We can have it settled by the end of the week if you're willing to accept the offer." Barbara spread the papers over the table, and the four of them looked them over together. An hour later, Morgan had signed off on everything she'd brought and agreed to come work on the rest of the paperwork the next day.

"Can I ask who bought it?" Morgan said as Barbara went to take her leave.

"I'm not sure," she replied, curiously. "It was an anonymous buyer." Morgan pondered on the idea for a moment and shrugged, giving Barbara a wave as she hopped into her car and took off down the road.

"I think this calls for a drink!" Abigail said, smiling happily.

As promised, the sale went through at the end of the week. Oddly enough, the process went far quicker than Morgan would have ever imagined it would. After Barbara met with her in the morning, Morgan took off to the other end of town to a neighborhood outside of Portland. It was beautiful and right on the coastline. The houses were modest and newer. Morgan had picked one in a cul-de-sac, right on the coast. There was even a new dock that had been built right out onto the water from the backyard.

The builders were working on finishing touches as Morgan pulled up. She'd visited every day since she found it and they'd gotten used to her showing up. Bill, the foreman, gave her a wave when he saw her. She wandered inside, taking in the large windows and spectacular views. It was a nice cottage style home.

"Have you told your girl yet?" Bill asked as he had her sign some final paperwork.

"Not yet," Morgan replied, scribbling her signature over a few pages. When she handed it back to him, he smiled.

"I'm sure she's gonna love it."

Morgan sure hoped so. "Can I have you guys do one more thing before you finish up?" She handed him the swatches that Abigail had helped her pick out. Three different colors of red. "Would you mind painting the front door for me?"

———————

MORGAN HAD LOADED THE last of the boxes into the truck the following week. They managed to fit perfectly. Abigail and Richard had run to get lunch. It was the first time all morning she had been left alone with the empty lighthouse. Morgan wandered back inside, a wave of emotions hitting her. Her hands traced along the walls, walking the length of the house. Finally, she found herself heading up the stairs to the top of the lighthouse.

It was a breezy fall afternoon. The trees were all sorts of beautiful colors. They made a canvas of oranges and reds and yellows with the choppy blues and whites of the ocean. Morgan opened one of the windows, breathing in the cool salty air. The idea that this would be the last time she'd sit here, admiring this view, was bittersweet, to say the least. As much as she was sad about the idea, the thought of surprising Lily in a few short hours was enough to ease her.

"Hey," a voice from behind her interrupted her thoughts. Morgan nearly lept through the window. Behind her, Lily stood at the foot of the stairs. She was the most beautiful sight that Morgan had ever seen. Her wispy, wavy hair wrapped around her face and her lips were curved into an enchanting smile. Morgan was still panting when she came to sit beside her. "You're an easy scare."

Morgan hugged her tightly, and Lily hugged her back. They stayed that way for a long while before Morgan finally pulled away. "What are you doing here?"

"I heard you sold the lighthouse," Lily said, a curious look on her face.

"I did," Morgan replied. Before she could continue the thought, Lily placed a finger to her lips with a smile.

"Before you say anything, I have something I need you to do." Lily took her by the hand and led her back down the stairs. Morgan followed quietly, unsure of what to think. When they made their way back into the house, Morgan saw the photo almost immediately, hanging on the empty wall by the front door. She turned to Lily, a questionable look spread across her face.

"What's going on, Lily?"

"Morgan," Lily said, taking her hand and looking up at the two-year-old picture of the starfish hanging on the wall. "Make a wish."

The Book

THE FIRST TIME LILY Taylor knew she wanted to marry Morgan Wallace, was at an estate sale on the outskirts of Portland. Morgan had always been a fan of yard sales and antiques, but Lily couldn't understand the appeal. She'd humored her anyway, and the two set off early on a Saturday morning in the spring.

"I still don't get why we're going to *this* specific house," Lily said as they turned off the main road into the neighborhood. "And why we had to get up so incredibly early," Lily yawned. Morgan had a suspicious look on her face and didn't answer. When they pulled into the driveway, it looked as if they were the first people there. Morgan parked the car, and the two of them headed up to the door.

The house had belonged to an older woman who had passed away a few weeks prior. It was a gorgeous colonial style home that she had lived in by herself. As soon as Morgan explained that she had been a librarian, Lily knew exactly why they had come.

The book collection was exquisite. While John and her father had collected many over the years, nothing compared to the hundreds and hundreds she had. Lily spent the morning pulling book after book off of shelves until she had gathered so many she could hardly carry them. Just as they were about to leave and pay for the lot, an unusual book caught her eye.

It was intricately bound, with a gold spine and brilliant emerald green lettering. The cover looked old and worn. Well-loved. Yet it wasn't the book itself that caught Lily's eye, but the title. An old EE Cummings anthology. After she'd handed the collection of items she had to Morgan, she carefully plucked it off the shelf, thumbing through it.

167

"Let's get this one too," Lily said, throwing it on the stack. Morgan and Lily paid for the goods and headed back out to the car.

The whole drive home, Lily was in an impeccable mood. As they pulled into the driveway of the lighthouse, she leaned over, planting a kiss on Morgan's cheek. "You are the best thing that ever happened to me."

That night, after Morgan had gone to bed, Lily found herself wide awake and unable to sleep. All she could think about was proposing to Morgan. She'd make a special day of it. They could go out on the boat. Lily imagined no more perfect way of asking than out on the water.

While she sat daydreaming, she thumbed through the stack of books from the estate sale. When she stumbled across the EE Cummings anthology, she took pause, setting it into her lap. As she opened it up to the title page, she let out a sharp gasp. Signed across the top in his unmistakable handwriting, was Cummings name.

Chapter Ten
Lily

IF IT HADN'T BEEN FOR her brother, Lily might have never left the bed that first week after she'd left the lighthouse. All the strength she had mustered over the months had dissipated. Between the fight with Morgan and the news about her spine, Lily barely was able to function. Luckily John proved to be a good distraction.

Four days after Lily had moved in, John took her out in the evening. There was no explanation of where only the promise that it wasn't an ambush by Morgan. They made their way all the way to Portland, keeping mostly to themselves as John drove. When they pulled up to an old shady looking building, Lily exchanged a curious look with her brother.

"Just trust me," John said as he hopped from the car. Before they went inside, he turned to look at her again. "I need you to promise me that you'll at least stay one time. No matter what happens."

Lily stared at him, unsure of what to think. "Stay where?"

"Just promise me," John repeated, and Lily nodded.

"I promise."

The room John led her to was full of a collection of people. Lily and her brother sat down just as a woman began to speak. She realized when she did that this was the last place she wanted to be.

"Good evening," the woman spoke. "I'm Tara. Thanks everyone for coming to the group."

Lily started to stand when she felt her brother grasp her wrist. Slowly she sat back down in the chair again, giving him a dirty look. He didn't pay her any mind, turning his attention towards Tara.

The intimate group went around the circle, introducing themselves one by one. When they reached John, he smiled and talked a little bit about himself. Then he looked at Lily. "I came here to support my sister."

All eyes were on Lily then, and she could feel her chest sink into her body. She took a deep breath before she spoke. "My name is Lily Taylor." At first, she thought that was all she would say, but before she knew it, she kept speaking. "Several months ago I was in a boating accident that caused me to lose my memory and some of my ability to walk." Even while she felt choked up saying it, it was equally a relief to admit it.

Most of the meeting hardly focused on her. Instead, she listened to others. Steve, a veteran amputee that had lost a leg in a landmine explosion while he was on tour in Iraq. Kristina, a mother of two who was battling breast cancer. Robert, who was recently diagnosed with MS.

By the end of the meeting, Lily found herself feeling more at ease than she had felt since the fight with Morgan. Since the news about her spine. She and John spent over an hour socializing afterward, and Lily had agreed with Tara that she would come the following week again.

On the way home, John and Lily talked like they hadn't in years. Lily felt strangely empowered. Just as they were pulling into the subdivision, her mood shifted. Suddenly a wave of sadness overcame her.

"I'm sorry, John," Lily said, turning to look at him.

After John parked the car in the driveway, he met eyes with her. "Why are you sorry?"

"I'm sorry for making you worry so much," Lily replied, wiping her eyes with the back of her hand. "I'm sorry that I made a stupid decision to go out on the boat that night and that I nearly got myself killed. I'm sorry you had to worry about losing me and having to go through all of those feelings again. I don't think I've told you that, and I've meant to."

John leaned over to take her hand. He squeezed it softly, smiling at her. "Lil, I'm going to worry about you regardless what happens. That's just how it goes."

"But after everything with Mom and Dad," Lily argued.

"Sure, that makes it more difficult," John agreed. "But you're my baby sister. It doesn't matter what happens, it's all the same." He pondered for a moment, looking at her. "I get a little carried away sometimes. I probably shouldn't coddle you so much."

Lily laughed, wiping her face again. "Maybe just a little."

John smiled, reaching over to place his hand against her cheek. "I'll try to reign it in. But, regardless. I love you, and I'll always worry. You're just going to have to get used to that." Lily nodded, sniffling loudly. "Now come on," John said, turning off the engine of the car. "Elise made some sort of casserole she's dying for you to try."

The following week, Lily agreed to meet Bill and Ryan again at work. She'd finally decided to stop putting off getting started. John dropped her off early in the morning on Monday, and as soon as she'd gotten inside, Becky greeted her, bearing a tray full of brownies. Lily took some graciously and chowed down while she waited.

"It's so nice to see you back," Becky smiled at her.

"I'm glad to be here," Lily nodded. The two sat and made small talk, and Lily was quick to realize why she'd liked her so much. She was easy to chat with and a great listener. Lily felt like all she did the entire conversation was talk about herself while Becky listened. Finally, Bill and Ryan came to get her, and the three made their way to a conference room.

Bill had arranged a meeting with a professor at the University of Maine. He was waiting for them inside the room when they'd gotten there.

"Lily Taylor, I'd like you to meet Dr. Marty Schoen," Bill said as Lily stuck out her hand. "Marty specializes in Marine Biology at UM, and he's offered to take you under his wing."

"Pleasure to meet you, Lily," Dr. Schoen said as the two shook hands.

Marty had agreed to take Lily and get her up to speed on the year and a half of coursework she was missing. While he worked with her, Lily would work on various aspects of the projects she'd been helping on before she left, doing whatever she could handle.

"When can I start?" Lily asked once she'd gotten back to Bill's office.

"As soon as you want to," Bill replied with a smile.

"How about now?"

On Friday, Lily left work early to go to a physical therapy appointment with John. As they were turning off the highway to head back to the house, a sign caught her eye.

"Hey John, turn around," Lily said when they'd passed it. Her brother did as she asked without question. "Pull over for a second." Once the car had stopped on the edge of the road, Lily hopped from the car, much to John's disapproval. She grabbed her cane and walked the few hundred feet up to the sign. It was unmistakable. A For Sale sign. Except Lily could barely believe the words written under it.

"The Wallace Family Lighthouse," Lily said when she'd gotten back in the car with her brother. "Morgan is selling it."

John looked as surprised as she felt. The two sat in silence for a while as her brother backed onto the road and headed back to the house.

"I can't believe she's selling the lighthouse," Lily said in disbelief when they'd reached the driveway.

The minute Lily got home with her brother, she called the number from the sign. After a few rings, a woman answered. "Sanford Realty, this is Barbara. How can I help you?"

"Yes, I'm calling about the Wallace Lighthouse," Lily said quickly. "I need to know if it's had any offers."

"And you are?"

"An interested buyer," Lily said the first thing that came to mind.

"Well, I'm afraid you just missed the opportunity," Barbara said, and Lily felt her heart sink into her chest. "The owner accepted an offer for the property this morning."

"An offer? From who?"

"Excuse me? Who is this exactly?"

"My name is Lily Taylor," Lily explained and before she could stop herself she'd told her everything. By the end, the line was silent, and Lily wasn't sure if she'd hung up or was still there.

"Sweetheart, I'm so sorry. There's nothing that can be done at this point."

"Nothing?" Lily pleaded, unsure of what else to do. Every part of her was aching.

"Not unless the buyer falls through, which is highly unlikely. She was very excited about turning the place into a bed and breakfast." Bed and breakfast. Lily felt sick to her stomach. Why on earth Morgan would do such a thing was beyond her.

"That property is a historical landmark," Lily argued. "It's been in the Wallace family for generations."

Barbara hesitated. "Nothing is protecting it from being used as a different type of property. Unless the historical society wanted to purchase it, there's nothing that can be done."

Frustrated, Lily thanked her for her time and hung up the phone. She sat for a long time, stretched out on her bed. After a few minutes, John came in and laid beside her.

"There's nothing I can do," Lily sighed, frustrated. "She sold it to some woman who wants to turn it into a glorified hotel." She felt herself on the verge of tears. The whole situation was likely her own fault. Morgan would have never dreamed to sell the lighthouse had it not been for her.

"What about Jacob?" John asked, looking towards her. When they met eyes, Lily studied him curiously.

"Jacob?"

"Jacob Elkins," John said. "You should talk to Jacob."

―――――――――

THE LAST TIME LILY had been to the Kennebunkport Historical Society, she'd been a young child. She barely remembered anything about the place. Jacob, the president, was thrilled when she'd asked to meet up with him again, and sensing her urgency, met her the following morning.

"So how can I help you?" Jacob said, taking a sip of the tea that his wife Annabelle had prepared for the two of them.

Lily cleared her throat, feeling rather awkward about the whole situation. She was here now. There was no turning back. "Well, I know the Historical Society sometimes looks into purchasing property around the area when it's of historical significance." Jacob raised a brow curiously. "I think I might know of a piece of property that would be of interest to you."

Jacob looked somewhat intrigued as he sat down his drink. Lily continued. "I'm not sure if you know, but the Wallace Family Lighthouse has been put up for sale."

"The one down south?" Jacob asked, and Lily nodded.

"I don't know if it would be possible, but I was just thinking.. It's been a landmark for the city for over a century." Lily found herself repeating almost verbatim the same speech Morgan gave to the visitors at the lighthouse, surprising herself how much she remembered. "I just think maybe, the society should consider purchasing it. Given its historical significance."

There was a silence in the room for a while as Jacob processed what Lily had said. She twiddled her fingers nervously as she waited for him to speak, unsure if she had made the right decision to even ask or not.

"While I think that is a spectacular idea, I'm not sure if we'd have the capability of doing that at the moment," Jacob admitted. Lily felt her heart sink into her chest when he said it. "I will think about it, however." She nodded, taking another sip of her tea. It was the last they discussed about it before Jacob made small talk with her until they'd both finished their drinks.

As Lily gathered her things, Jacob caught her by the arm. "So, I'm curious, if you wouldn't mind humoring an old man for a minute." Lily met eyes with him, and he smiled. "Why all the interest in the Wallace Lighthouse?"

"I'd do just about anything for the woman who lives there," Lily admitted, unable to help herself thinking about Morgan. Even through all her frustration, she still meant what she said.

Jacob nodded, and Lily shouldered her purse, following him as he led her to the front door.

"Tell your brother I said hello," Jacob said, shaking her hand. Lily nodded and headed out the door to call him.

AS MUCH AS LILY HATED waking up early on the weekend, she reasoned with herself to go with John to the bookstore. It was a much-needed distraction after the disappointing day with the historical society. The whole morning she fought the urge to call Morgan. Guilt still plagued her from the situation. She'd call eventually when this all settled down.

The bookstore, which was usually quiet on Sundays, was surprisingly busy. John kept Lily working most of the day, ringing up orders and stocking shelves. When things quieted down in the afternoon, Lily found herself wandering down aisles of the used books. As she passed the EE Cummings book on the wall, she took it down from its case, thumbing through it carefully. Her fingers lightly brushed over the signature in awe.

As she sifted through the pages, she happened upon her favorite poem. Her father's favorite. The first she'd ever heard by EE Cummings. She read it quietly to herself, pausing at the end.

"For whatever we lose (like a you or a me), it's always ourselves we find in the sea."

That night at dinner, as John talked with Elise about the busy and eventful day they'd had at the bookstore, Lily took careful note of him. His wide and thoughtful eyes and his peaceful smile. The way his body moved when he spoke about it. Everything he did reminded Lily of how Morgan spoke when she'd talk about the lighthouse. Suddenly Lily couldn't imagine Morgan ever giving it up.

"John," Lily said when he'd finished. "I think I want to do something kind of crazy."

An hour later they arrived at Jacob's doorstep, Lily clutching the much-loved EE Cummings anthology in her arms. When Annabelle answered, Lily and John were ushered inside. Jacob met them in his study, and the three sat down together.

"John, what a pleasant surprise," Jacob said, shaking his hand.

"Glad to see you again," John replied with a smile.

"I need to ask you to reconsider," Lily said, looking at Jacob. "The lighthouse. I need you to buy it from Morgan Wallace."

"I must say, Ms. Taylor, you are the most persistent person I've ever met." Jacob took a seat and met her gaze. Lily smiled at him for a moment before she handed him the book. Jacob took it carefully from her, studying it for a moment. "This is the book from your bookstore. The autographed anthology."

"I want you to have it," Lily said, firmly.

"I couldn't possibly," Jacob tried to hand it back to her, and she refused.

"Hear me out," Lily argued, and Jacob rested the book in his lap, carefully. "I want you to have it. My father would have wanted you to have it. In my mind, no better person would love that book than an academic of history and literature." Jacob stared at her curiously, and she continued.

"But you have to understand. The Wallace Lighthouse isn't just a building. I know you know that. It's a monument. A historical landmark. A place that needs to be protected. I could sit with you and explain all day about how much that property means to the Wallace family, but in the end, it should be just as important to the city to preserve it. Like how it is important to preserve that book." Lily went on to explain about Morgan's plans to make it volunteer run. By the end of it, Lily was almost certain she had him convinced until he spoke.

"I know how much it means to you," Jacob finally said, and Lily felt her heart sink. "I'll have to talk to the board in the morning, but I'm still not sure it's possible. Especially given such a small time-frame."

Lily nodded. All she could do at this point was try.

"MAKE A WISH," LILY said as she stood under the starfish with Morgan. She found herself thinking about that chilly evening on the sidewalk when they'd first saw the photo. Morgan stared at her for a long time, unsure of what to say. Lily nudged her, and she closed her eyes, pondering for a moment. When she opened them again, Lily smiled.

"I did something crazy," Morgan admitted when she turned to look at her.

"Me too," Lily smiled at her and just as she did she saw the car pull up to the driveway. "Come on." Lily took Morgan by the hand and led her outside.

"There's someone I want you to meet," Lily turned to Morgan, as Jacob got out of his car and walked over. "This is Jacob Elkins."

Morgan stood confused as Jacob shook her hand. "I've heard a lot about you the past few days," Jacob smiled.

"Jacob bought the lighthouse," Lily said, and Morgan's face turned surprised.

"Technically the Kennebunkport Historical Society bought the lighthouse," Jacob corrected her. "Lily tells me you're well versed in the lightkeeping business."

Morgan nodded, at a loss for what to say. Lily couldn't help but smile at her.

"We'd like to offer you a job," Jacob said, looking up at the building and shading his eyes from the sunlight.

"A job?" Morgan repeated.

"Running the volunteer program at the Wallace Lighthouse. We couldn't think of a better person to do it," Jacob offered a smile. "Given the fact, you're a Wallace, and this was your lighthouse..."

Morgan braced herself on Lily's shoulder. "It's not going to be a bed and breakfast?"

Lily laughed and leaned over to kiss her on the cheek.

After the meeting with Jacob, Morgan loaded Lily into her car, along with the starfish photo. When Lily asked where they were going, Morgan only smiled. "I didn't get my wish," she replied as they headed down the road.

"I thought you'd wish that you could keep the lighthouse," Lily said, surprised.

They drove for over an hour, passing through the outskirts of Portland and driving along the coast. When they reached a small subdivision, Morgan pulled over in front of a row of houses.

Lily followed her up the walkway of a cute blue and white cottage house. When she saw the front door, painted a poppy shade of red, Lily felt tears streaming down her face.

Morgan and Lily hung the starfish photo together. They spent the afternoon stretched out on blankets and pillows on the living room floor. When Morgan made peanut butter and jelly sandwiches for dinner, Lily split them down the middle, and then the two went to the dock to eat. As the sun was setting and the sky filled with brilliant pink and purple hues, Lily knew Morgan was staring at her.

When she turned, Lily gasped softly. In between Morgan's fingers was a simple gold band engagement ring. It glistened in the remainder of the sunlight. She took it carefully. The two of them met eyes, and Morgan smiled. "Do you want to know what I wished for?"

Epilogue
Morgan

IT WAS AN EARLY SPRING morning in Kennebunkport. The trees were in bloom, and the wind picked up the scent of the maples as they drove down the coastal road. Lily's head was leaning out of the passenger side of the car as they made their way onto the gravel path leading up to the Wallace Family Lighthouse. There were dozens of people that had already gathered. Morgan could feel a pit growing in her stomach as she parked the car.

Before they exited, she felt Lily's hand wrap around her own. Morgan turned to look at her, smiling. As simple as a gesture as it was, Lily had always known exactly how to calm her. "This is your day. You're going to be great," Lily said, leaning over to kiss her softly.

Just as they exited the car, Richard and Abigail met them, crossing the road. It had been a while since they'd last seen one another. They chatted while they walked towards the lighthouse. Lily had gotten exceptionally good at walking with her cane. It had almost become natural.

"We'll drop by for dessert later," Morgan promised Abigail as they broke apart. As soon as they started to walk away, she spotted John standing in the crowd with Elise and their two sons. Lily met her brother and sister-in-law, hugging them. Morgan followed suit.

"A little nervous there, are you?" John said, and Morgan rolled her eyes.

"John!" Lily scolded, nudging him in the side.

John gave Morgan a smile, and she relaxed. She picked up Ian from the stroller and snuggled him for a moment, while Lily held Thomas.

When they were through, Morgan offered a hug to Elise before she turned to Lily.

"You're going to do great," she whispered, leaning over to kiss her softly on the lips. Morgan couldn't help but smile and rest a hand on her cheek.

"I don't know what I'd do without you," she whispered before they parted.

Jacob Elkins met Morgan at the entrance, just as people had gathered around. There must have been fifty by then. Morgan tried not to focus on that, instead looking into the crowd for Lily.

"Well, I guess I'll get started," Jacob said, interrupting the murmuring voices. "We want to thank you all for coming today. As most of you are aware, last year the Kennebunkport Historical Society purchased this monumental piece of property. After some hard work and determination, we're proud to make this the official beginning of the volunteer program for the Wallace Family Lighthouse."

"I'm going to let Morgan Wallace, the manager of the program, say a few words before we do the ribbon cutting."

Jacob looked to Morgan, who fidgeted with the notecards she'd pulled from her pocket. When she looked out at the crowd, she lost her breath. She turned to look up at the lighthouse and found the moment of fear quickly passing. As she looked back, she smiled, pocketing the cards.

"Sixty-five years ago, my grandfather, Patrick Wallace, received the deed to a lighthouse in Maine. The Wallace Family Lighthouse had survived four generations before him and even as rickety and old as it was back then, my grandfather loved it with all his heart.

He used to say that lighthouses don't save ships; they don't go out and rescue them. It's just the pillar that helps to guide people home.

This lighthouse gave me years of memories with my grandfather, with my family, with the love of my life. I hope it will bring this city and the volunteers who run it the same memories." She looked out at Lily, smiling as she took a step back. Jacob came to speak again, and Morgan felt a wave of emotion wash over her. "Wait," she said, grasping a hold of his wrist.

"Lily Taylor," Morgan called out to the crowd for her. When people turned to look, Lily blushed at the attention. "Will you marry me today?"

Lily stared at her stunned. For a minute Morgan wasn't sure if she'd made the right decision until Lily began to walk through the crowd towards her. They met together at the foot of the lighthouse, Lily laughing and crying simultaneously.

A small crowd of people came with Lily and Morgan to the Portland courthouse that afternoon. John, Elise, and the boys. Abigail and Richard. Much to Lily's surprise, Morgan even called her parents while they were driving. It was a quick and simple ceremony, filled with Lily's happy tears, John's intermittent jokes, and Morgan's loving words. Before they left, John broke open a bottle of champagne, and they all shared in a toast.

Morgan looked at Lily before she spoke. At those soft, beautiful gray eyes that had captivated her since she was a little girl. The smile that had welcomed her that day in third-grade. The smile that had since never made her feel alone. Morgan looked at her best friend, the love of her life, and she knew. At the very heart of things, at the core, we are who we are. We love who we love. And there is nothing in the world that will ever change that.

Made in the USA
San Bernardino, CA
01 March 2018